The dragon  **on Zakynthos's black hair glitter in the light, reminding me of my plan, which is, in essence, very simple.**

Her brother took my family from me and so I will take his family from him. I will take her, turn her against him, make her mine and then, once she is, I will take his company too.

It won't be difficult to get close to her. The information I've gathered so far indicates she's been sheltered all her life so she'll have no protections from a man like me. She'll fall to me as all the rest have fallen, willingly and happily, but...

I have to admit, I didn't expect her to be so lovely or for my body to instinctively tighten at the sight of her. Beautiful women I can get with a snap of my fingers, yet there's something about this one, something I can't name, that digs deep inside me and pulls. The way she's standing with her elbows on the rail, staring at the view. The way her eyes are wide and her lovely mouth curves, as if she's never seen a view like this one before.

A shockingly spicy new duet from Jackie Ashenden!

Captured and Claimed

If passion can't be contained...it must be controlled!

Ruthless Greek billionaire Ulysses Zakynthos lives by one rule: that you can never have too much money, power or influence. That's how he insulates himself and his sister, Olympia, from the pain of their childhood. There's nothing he wouldn't do to protect his family.

Yet, in all the years he's been building his empire, no one has ever challenged his belief system like Katla Sigurdsdottir. She fascinates him. And he has to have her... The only way to do that is by proving her need for him is as great as his own!

Read Ulysses and Katla's story in

Christmas Eve Ultimatum

Olympia Zakynthos was a means to an end for Rafael Santangelo. His seduction of her will be his revenge for her brother's ruthless takeover of his family's business. Only revenge has bound them together in the most permanent way of all... She's expecting the Sicilian's baby!

Discover Olympia's story in

His Heir of Revenge

Both available now!

HIS HEIR OF REVENGE

JACKIE ASHENDEN

PRESENTS

If you purchased this book without a cover you should be aware that this book is stolen property. It was reported as "unsold and destroyed" to the publisher, and neither the author nor the publisher has received any payment for this "stripped book."

MIX
Paper | Supporting responsible forestry
FSC® C021394

Recycling programs for this product may not exist in your area.

ISBN-13: 978-1-335-21341-9

His Heir of Revenge

Copyright © 2025 by Jackie Ashenden

All rights reserved. No part of this book may be used or reproduced in any manner whatsoever without written permission.

Without limiting the exclusive rights of any author, contributor or the publisher of this publication, any unauthorized use of this publication to train generative artificial intelligence (AI) technologies is expressly prohibited. Harlequin also exercises their rights under Article 4(3) of the Digital Single Market Directive 2019/790 and expressly reserves this publication from the text and data mining exception.

This is a work of fiction. Names, characters, places and incidents are either the product of the author's imagination or are used fictitiously. Any resemblance to actual persons, living or dead, businesses, companies, events or locales is entirely coincidental.

For questions and comments about the quality of this book, please contact us at CustomerService@Harlequin.com.

TM and ® are trademarks of Harlequin Enterprises ULC.

Harlequin Enterprises ULC
22 Adelaide St. West, 41st Floor
Toronto, Ontario M5H 4E3, Canada
www.Harlequin.com

HarperCollins Publishers
Macken House, 39/40 Mayor Street Upper,
Dublin 1, D01 C9W8, Ireland
www.HarperCollins.com

Printed in Lithuania

Jackie Ashenden writes dark, emotional stories with alpha heroes who've just gotten the world to their liking only to have it blown apart by their kick-ass heroines. She lives in Auckland, New Zealand, with her husband, the inimitable Dr. Jax, two kids and two rats. When she's not torturing alpha males and their gutsy heroines, she can be found drinking chocolate martinis, reading anything she can lay her hands on, wasting time on social media or being forced to go mountain biking with her husband. To keep up-to-date with Jackie's new releases and other news, sign up to her newsletter at jackieashenden.com.

Books by Jackie Ashenden

Harlequin Presents

A Vow to Redeem the Greek
Spanish Marriage Solution
Newlywed Enemies
King, Enemy, Husband

The Teras Wedding Challenge

Enemies at the Greek Altar

Scandalous Heirs

Italian Baby Shock
The Twins That Bind

Work Wives to Billionaires' Wives

Boss's Heir Demand

Captured and Claimed

Christmas Eve Ultimatum

Visit the Author Profile page
at Harlequin.com for more titles.

This one is for our visitors from the Mount.
You know who you are.

CHAPTER ONE

Rafael

I SEE HER leaning against the rail that bounds the SkyPark Observation deck, one of the most unique buildings in Singapore. Her black hair is twisted up into an elegant knot at the back of her head and adorned with jewelled hair clips in the shape of dragonflies. Her gown is scarlet silk, wrapped around her slender figure in a complicated series of twists that highlight the luscious curves of breasts, hips and thighs.

The humid, scented air toys with the split in her dress, revealing one rounded thigh and making the silk billow around her legs. She wears matching high-heeled sandals of scarlet silk with straps that criss-cross up her calves, making her legs look long and elegant.

This building is an architectural marvel, but she… is a masterpiece. Clean and precise in her nose, cheekbones, jaw. Yet also sensual with that sulky, delicious mouth and delicately arched, dark brows.

She's looking at the view, her eyes wide, a rapt expression on her lovely face. It's true, the view is spectacular, but I don't care about the view. At least not of the city or the harbour. The view I'm particularly concerned about tonight is the woman leaning up against the rail.

She's why I'm here, but she's not what I expected, not in any way.

She's Olympia Zakynthos, the younger sister of the one man I hate above all others—Ulysses Zakynthos, owner of the huge energy conglomerate Vulcan Energy. A powerful man. Also, the man directly responsible for the ruination of my family's company and my family along with it.

It's been years since that happened, and in that time I've slowly but surely made a name for myself and Atlas Construction, the construction company that I started as a labourer in and now am the CEO of. I've also made many plans for how to best get my revenge on the man who caused my father's death and my mother to sell herself to pay his debts. Yet the time and circumstances have never been right.

However, Sicilians like their revenge served cold, and I am Sicilian through and through, and now, finally, it's the right time and the path to my revenge is standing in front of me, leaning against the rail and admiring the view.

Ulysses Zakynthos's Achilles heel. His only weakness.

The occasion is a charitable gala for the very rich and powerful, so, after my sources informed me that Vulcan Energy would be represented, not by Ulysses, but by his younger sister, I made sure to secure an invite.

I'm not well liked by high society—I'm too raw,

too rough, too unrefined and unsophisticated for their tastes—but that doesn't bother me. Nothing bothers me, nothing except the loathing in my heart for the man who ruined me.

The dragonflies in Olympia Zakynthos's black hair glitter in the light, drawing my attention back to her, reminding me of my plan, which is, in essence, very simple. Her brother took my family from me and so I will take his family from him. I will take her, turn her against him, make her mine and then, once she is, I will take his company too.

It won't be difficult to get close to her. The information I've gathered so far indicates she's been sheltered all her life so she'll have no protections from a man like me. And I know women. I know what they like and I know what gets them off. To say my experience is wide and free-ranging would be to understate the case, so I'm sure I won't have any problems seducing Miss Olympia Zakynthos. She'll fall to me as all the rest have fallen, willingly and happily, but…

I have to admit, I didn't expect her to be so lovely or for my body to instinctively tighten at the sight of her. Beautiful women I can get with a snap of my fingers, yet there's something about this one, something I can't name, that digs deep inside me and pulls. The way she's standing with her elbows on the rail, staring at the view. The way her eyes are wide and her lovely mouth curves, as if she's never seen a view like this one before. It speaks of…innocence almost.

I can work with that.

The other guests swirl around me as I grab two

glasses of excellent champagne from a passing waiter. Then I move over to where my quarry is standing.

She doesn't notice me, a wolf moving amongst the sheep and approaching the smallest of lambs, ready to devour. She has no idea that tonight she will cause her brother's ruin. However, just before I arrive at her side some sort of sixth sense alerts her, a latent survival instinct detecting the approach of a predator, and she turns her head suddenly, her gaze meeting mine.

The impact of those amber eyes is almost physical and I stop dead in my tracks, the champagne in my glass sloshing against the rim as I nearly spill it.

Dio. I have never seen eyes that colour, a delicate, smoky gold, but something in them pierces me like a crossbow bolt. I'm caught, held there, staring at her like a teenage boy poleaxed by his first sight of a girl in a bikini.

The air between us seethes with electricity. It almost suffocates me. Then her thick, black silky lashes fall, veiling her gaze as colour washes through her cheeks, and a powerful satisfaction seizes me.

I was never in doubt that she'd find me attractive—most women do, after all—yet seeing the confirmation on her face is a drug I can't resist.

Like a magnet I'm drawn to her, so I continue on, coming up to the rail beside her and holding out the glass of champagne. 'Such a beautiful view deserves the best champagne, don't you think?' I say in Greek, her mother tongue. I make sure she knows which particular view I'm talking about.

Those silky lashes lift and, again, her incredible eyes meet mine.

Dio, she's luminous.

A hesitant smile curves her mouth and it's so unbelievably sweet my cold, dead heart catches in my chest.

'Oh,' she says, the most delicious husk in her clear voice. 'You speak Greek? Thank God. My English isn't bad, but I keep making such an idiot of myself. Wait…' Her eyes widen. 'How do you know I'm Greek?'

Fuck.

I've given myself away. I shouldn't know who she is, let alone that she's Greek, but she had me so transfixed I spoke without thinking. That won't happen again.

I'm good at hiding what I feel, I always have been. Emotions are a weakness I can't afford, not in the cut-throat world that I was forced into years ago, as a *Cosa Nostra* enforcer, and not in business either. So I don't let a hint of her effect on me show as I gather my resources to respond. Conversation is not a forte of mine, nor do I enjoy it. I prefer action to pretty words. But women sometimes require pretty words so I merely smile back at her. 'Because you're Olympia Zakynthos,' I say easily. 'Head of Vulcan Energy, no?'

Pink flushes the delicate olive skin of her cheeks. 'Yes, but I'm not the head of Vulcan Energy. That's my brother, Ulysses. I'm only representing him at the gala tonight.'

'Surely not "only",' I murmur.

The pretty smile plays around her luscious mouth. 'Oh, believe me, it definitely is "only". He's back in Athens.' She waves a hand. 'Doing something with something.' Immediately the words come out of her mouth, she flushes again and a soft, self-conscious laugh breaks from her. 'Sorry, that sounds stupid. The truth is, this is my first social occasion on my own for...ages. I'm not used to so many people I don't know and, also, I'm terrible at small talk.'

I don't want to be charmed by her honesty and yet, against my will, I am. 'I don't blame you,' I say. 'I don't find social occasions easy, either. To that end, allow me to introduce myself. I am Rafael Santangelo.' I extend the champagne to her again. 'There. Now you know one person at least.'

The gold of her eyes glows as she takes the champagne flute from me, and I can't resist making sure the tips of my fingers brush hers as she does so. Her gaze flares as we touch and I hear the slight catch of her breath, feel the prickle of undeniable electricity that chases over my skin.

Dio, I wasn't expecting attraction to spark between us so quickly, but I'm not unhappy with the situation. It will make my job so much easier.

'Pleased to meet you, Rafael Santangelo,' she says, giving me an adorable mock bow. Then she looks pointedly at the glass of champagne I'm presenting her with. 'I should warn you that my brother has told me not to accept drinks from strange men.'

I lean against the rail, still holding the wretched glasses. She's not very tall. The top of her head only reaches my shoulder. 'But I'm not a strange man,' I say. 'You know my name.'

Her smile is a delight. A gift that she's giving and

only to me. 'That's true. And you know mine, so I suppose we're hardly strangers.'

She takes the glass from me without a second's thought and an unfamiliar part of me wants to snatch it back from her, tell her that her brother is right, she shouldn't be accepting drinks from strange men. Especially men like me. I once helped the local *consiglieri* run protection rackets, a gun in my hand to enforce compliance, my fists and a knife to mete out punishments. People were afraid of me, as they should be. And so should she.

'If you like,' I say before she can take a sip, prompted by this odd protective urge, 'I could go and get you another glass and you could watch me to make sure there's nothing in the drink.'

'You could,' she agrees, then tilts her head, surveying me, assessing me as if I'm a threat. And I am. A little lamb like her should be running for the hills, yet instead, she smiles. 'It's okay. I trust you.' She nods her head to a man standing alone in the crowd not too far away. 'I have a bodyguard. He's there to rescue me from the consequences of my own idiocy.'

I know she has a bodyguard. I've already noted him and dismissed him as no danger to me or my plan. But her openness and willingness to trust is unexpected and presents an…unexpected obstacle. I want to tell her that trusting me is the last thing she should do, but I bite down on the urge. I have a revenge plan to follow and she is the key. A key I can't afford to throw away.

'You seem very convinced of your idiocy,' I say. 'That's the second time you've mentioned it.'

She laughs and takes a sip of champagne, her nose wrinkling at the bubbles. Then she closes her eyes. 'Oh my God, you're right. I told you I wasn't used to people.' Her eyes open again and she gives me a look from beneath her lashes. 'Sorry, I know I should be talking about how wonderful Vulcan Energy is and all of that, blah blah. But truth is, I know nothing about it. I'm only here for the holiday.'

Something rises in me, something fierce and protective. She shouldn't be so honest with a stranger. It's a mistake. It leaves a chink in your amour, makes you vulnerable. And she, so beautiful and so honest, should not be so vulnerable.

Especially when I am around.

'And why are you not used to people?' I ask, ruthlessly exploiting her weakness, because that's the kind of man I am. Ruthless.

She sighs, and leans on the rail beside me, mimicking my stance. 'Oh, truth is, I don't go out a lot. This is my first visit to Singapore. In fact, it's my first visit anywhere.'

Interesting. Another little fact to file away.

'What do you think of it so far?' I ask.

'It's so beautiful.' She glances out over the view once again. 'The gardens and the fountains, the harbour...' Her gaze comes back to mine, a spark of mischief in it that renders me momentarily speechless. 'What I really wanted to do was have a Singapore Sling in the Raffles Hotel. But Georgios over there has strict instructions from my brother that I'm not allowed to go out on my own.'

I knew she would not be unprotected. What I didn't know was that she would find that constraining herself.

'Surely Georgios can take you to Raffles,' I say casually, privately wondering how anyone could refuse this woman anything.

'Oh, he could,' Olympia replies. 'But I want to go by myself, without him. He's like a…a dark cloud hovering everywhere. Kind of spoils the vibe.'

'Can you not send him away?'

She sighs. 'He takes orders from my brother, not me, so no. Ulysses is so overprotective it's ridiculous.'

While she might not be able to see why her brother is overprotective, I do. There is an innocence to her, a guilelessness matched only by a smile so bright it hurts. She's like the sun, a light I'm drawn to, and I won't be the only one. She's vulnerable, achingly, painfully vulnerable, and I'm a bastard for doing what I'm going to do to her.

I should walk away from her while I still can. She'll think me rude, perhaps even be slightly hurt, but…no. I'm not going to walk away. The damage her brother did was too great, and my fury at him is too strong.

I was the one who came home one day to find my father dead in his study with a gunshot wound to the head and blood everywhere after Ulysses destroyed his company. I was the one who had to deal with a hysterical mother unable to believe her husband took his own life. And I was the one who had to watch the debt collectors come and take everything in sight.

So no. There will be no baulking at the last hurdle. It's only her feelings that are at risk here, and I don't care about her feelings. I want my revenge and I will have it.

'You can't come all the way to Singapore and not have a drink at Raffles,' I say instead. 'I'll take you if you like.'

CHAPTER TWO

Olympia

I REALLY DON'T know what I'm doing, but I don't care. I didn't care the moment I saw him, a point of perfect stillness in the moving, swirling stream of guests at the gala. He was in severe black, unlike the rest of the crowd flitting around him like a host of brightly coloured tropical birds. The women in jewels and fabulous gowns, and the men, too, glittering.

I was feeling so out of my depth and then I saw him, coming towards me. His eyes were so dark, almost black, and the minute they met mine it felt as if the earth had shifted beneath my feet. It sounds ridiculous and fanciful, a cliche even, but it's true.

He was coming for me, I knew it instinctively and I had to look away, my face flaming, a wild excitement beginning to take hold of me.

I could sense him coming to a stop beside me at the rail, just as I could sense the pressure of his gaze on me. It made me feel hot, made me blush, made me want to do something wild and reckless, which isn't like me at all. And then he spoke, his voice deep and dark, his Greek tinged with the flavours of Italy, and I couldn't resist it. I had to look at him and when I did I felt something kick hard inside me.

He's the most utterly mesmerising man I've ever met, not that I've met very many men. At all. In fact, I can count the number of men I've met since living with my brother on one hand.

Still, I'm sure that, not only is Rafael Santangelo the most mesmerising man I've ever met, he's probably the most mesmerising man I will *ever* meet.

He's very tall, probably my brother's height, which is six four, and he's built broad. Wide shoulders and muscled chest, like a warrior out of history. Achilles, maybe, or Hector. In fact, I can see him on an ancient battlefield with a horsehair-crested helmet, riding in a chariot with a spear in one large, long-fingered hand.

Except here, tonight, he's a modern warrior in his black evening clothes, and there are no frills or flounces about him, nothing glittering, and the asceticism suits him.

His features are rough and unfinished, yet there's something about his proud nose, heavy eyebrows and deep-set black eyes that is incredibly and powerfully magnetic. He has an aura, this man, of darkness and violence and something tells me he's very dangerous, but that only adds to his magnetism.

I've never been attracted to a man before. One of the 'perks' of being sheltered all my life by my brother. Ulysses means well and I know he does it because he loves me, because he blames himself for my dreadful childhood, but I'm getting tired of it. I've missed out on so many things a woman my age should have experienced by now. A career, friends, travel, and yes, a boyfriend.

I could leave, I know that, but I worry about him. I'm all he has and, considering that he rescued me from my abusive foster parents, cared for me in the aftermath, and gave me a home, I can't just abandon him.

Still, I've been nagging at him for months to at least bring me with him on his next business trip, but then he surprised me by suggesting I go to a special gala in Singapore as his representative. I was shocked at first, then thrilled, then actually quite annoyed when he said that, although he wouldn't be going, he would be assigning me a permanent security detail to accompany me.

That wasn't what I had in mind, of course, but arguing with Ulysses is always pointless. He never listens to me, telling me that my safety is the most important thing in his life and no way in hell is he putting that at risk.

It was either that or I didn't go, so in the end I had to accept the security.

It's not so bad tonight at the gala, because they're mingling with the guests and keeping a low profile, but I know they're there. I can feel them watching me and watching Rafael Santangelo too.

Nerves are coiling in my gut, along with a thrill of anticipation, and even though I've only had a couple of sips of champagne, I already feel dizzy. Perhaps there was something in that glass after all. Then again, some deep, instinctive part of me knows that there wasn't.

And I was telling him the truth when I told him that I trusted him.

Still, it's reckless of me to go anywhere with a man I only met two seconds ago. Ulysses would instantly forbid me. Then again, Ulysses isn't here and Rafael's offer is so tempting.

I study him, trying to sort out exactly what I'm feeling and why. Attraction is there, yes, I can feel that pulling me towards him like a magnet. A thrilling kind of fear too, but it's not a bad fear. It's a fear more akin to take-off in a plane, when you're barrelling so fast down the runway, ready to take flight, and you're helpless against the G-forces pushing you back in your seat.

Rafael Santangelo feels like one of those G-forces. Impossible to resist, an implacable gravity. I don't know why that makes me shiver, but it does, and I like the sensation. I like the way he's looking at me too, as if it's really me he's seeing. Ulysses doesn't see me. All he sees when he looks at me is his own guilt staring back at him.

There's no guilt in Rafael's dark eyes. His stare is… intense. Unwavering. It's as if he doesn't see anyone else at this gala but me and it's intoxicating. Once, when I was thirteen, I crept down into Ulysses's wine cellar and took a bottle of champagne. I drank half of it before being sick, but just before the sickness hit, I felt amazing. As if the bubbles in the wine had crept into my blood, making it fizz and pop in my veins.

I feel that same sensation now as he stares at me, and it's wonderful. It makes me realise how small and narrow my life has become, and gives me a glimpse of how much more it could be. How much more it *will* be.

'I'm not sure Georgios would approve,' I say, mock stern, my heartbeat accelerating with anticipation. I already know I'm going to take his offer and I don't care what Ulysses will say when he finds out.

'Fuck Georgios's approval,' Rafael murmurs, the pressure of his stare unrelenting.

There's a challenge in his eyes and I want to meet it with every part of me so I smile, unable to help myself. 'What about you? I wouldn't want to take you away from this very important gala.' I'm teasing and it feels a bit like I'm pulling on a tiger's tail, but that excitement is fizzing in my blood and it's overtaking me.

He continues to stare at me like a botanist examining some rare and precious undiscovered flower. 'I don't like galas,' he says. 'But I like you.'

It's such a simple sentence, yet I feel warmth bloom in my chest. He can't know me well enough to like me, not when we've only just met, but it makes me feel good all the same.

This is not a good idea.

Of course it isn't and I shouldn't even be contemplating it. Ulysses would have fifty fits if he knew what was happening. Then again, Ulysses has been controlling my life since I was ten years old and I'm tired of it, no matter how much I worry about him or how much I owe him. I'm tired of being Rapunzel in the tower and I want to escape. I want to let down my hair, have my prince find me, rescue me.

He is not a prince.

No, he's not. Even me, sheltered virgin that I am, can sense his dark aura, intense and cold and sharp, violent almost. He's an arrow flying towards a target and that target is me. It's an alarming thing to think yet I'm not alarmed. I'm thrilled.

Oh, Ulysses has told me all about the evils of men and certainly I remember how I was treated by my foster father. It's not as if I can forget that early part of my life. But not all men are evil, and I can't be imprisoned in my tower for ever. Rafael Santangelo, whether he knows it or not, has opened the door and I want to walk through it.

'I like you too,' I say, knowing even as I say it that I'm being too honest, too unguarded, which was another thing Ulysses told me not to be. 'But... I've only just met you.'

He smiles and my gaze is drawn by the curve of his mouth. The shape of it is cruel and yet when he smiles all I can see is the softness of his bottom lip. It makes me feel as if my heart is heating up from the inside. 'I don't want to make you uncomfortable,' he says. 'Tell Georgios he is welcome to accompany us so he knows where we're going.'

It's gallant of him and yet...it's not quite what I wanted.

'We can leave him at the door,' Rafael goes on, already seeing the expression on my face and instantly guessing the issue. 'It's very public inside the bar. There are lots of people around. We won't be alone together.'

A small thread of annoyance winds through my excitement. I appreciate his care for my comfort, but I'm tired of people being careful with me. I've been coddled and cosseted ever since Ulysses rescued me from the violence of my foster family. He treats me as if I'm made of china, a figurine to be kept in a glass cabinet and never taken out, never touched.

I know he means well, and it's not that I'm ungrateful for what he's done for me. But I don't want to be treated like that. What I want is to go to the famous hotel and have the famous drink with this incredibly attractive man.

'I bet serial killers say that,' I say. 'Before they serial kill.'

Something like surprise flashes through his dark eyes and then he laughs, and it's as if the sun has come out in the dead of night, warm and bright and shining down on me. 'I'm not a serial killer,' he says, still laughing. 'But I have to say, that's the first time I've been accused of being one.'

I don't know him at all yet I get the sense that he's not a man who smiles easily, and the fact that I've managed to get him to do so within seconds of meeting him makes me feel as if I've won a lottery.

'I could be a serial killer of serial killers,' I say, intoxicated with my own cleverness. 'So you might be in danger from me.'

Amusement glitters in his eyes and I feel very pleased with myself. 'That could be,' he says. 'Beautiful women wearing red silk are always very dangerous.'

Perhaps it's a practised compliment. Perhaps he says

things like that to women all the time, and yet I can't shake the sense that I surprised it out of him. Which makes me feel even more pleased with myself. I know Ulysses thinks I'm beautiful, but he's my big brother. He kind of has to say that. So coming from this man, this stranger, the compliment goes straight to my head as the champagne did.

'Come on, then.' Impulsively, I reach for his free hand. 'Let's go before Georgios says it's too late for me to leave.'

Yet more surprise flickers across his face as I thread my fingers through his, and then something hot blazes in his eyes, and for the first time I wonder if this is somehow a mistake. But then his large, warm hand grips mine, and every thought vanishes from my head, except for the knowledge that if this is a mistake then it's one I'm happy to make.

I put down my glass and move through the crowd, pulling Rafael along with me. We pass by Georgios, but I don't stop. 'Mr Santangelo is taking me to Raffles for a Singapore Sling,' I inform him over my shoulder.

Georgios says something, but I'm already past him and Rafael is no longer being pulled, but walking beside me. 'I have a car,' he says. 'I'll get the valet to bring it up.'

'Do you live here?' I ask him curiously as we take the lift to the parking level.

'No,' he says. 'My home is in Sicily. I am only here for the gala.'

Ah, so I was right about his accent. 'So why do you have a car?'

'I bought it yesterday,' he says. 'I like driving.'

'So you like me and you like driving. That's two things I know about you, which makes you definitely not a stranger any more. In fact, we're basically friends now.'

Something glitters in his dark eyes. 'I'm not your friend, dragonfly.'

There is something in his voice, something in his eyes, that makes me feel hot, as if my skin has suddenly become too hot and too tight. It sounds like a threat, yet I don't feel threatened. It's more as if he's issued me with a challenge.

'Dragonfly?' I arch a brow. 'Is that a special Sicilian thing?'

'No.' His gaze touches on my hair. 'Your hair clips.'

Oh, that's right. I forgot about those. I noticed them in a shop while I was sightseeing yesterday, and I thought they would go perfectly with the dress I was going to wear to the gala. I don't get the chance to dress up often and I always like it when I do. Pretty jewellery and pretty dresses and shoes are my weakness, and tonight I feel like a princess in my scarlet gown and jewelled clips.

I feel like a princess when Rafael stares at me too.

We arrive at the valet-parking area and don't have to wait long for Rafael to have his car brought around. I don't know what kind of car it is, but it's sleek and low-slung, and very beautiful. It's also the same shade of scarlet as my dress. The doors open like a bird's wings and I slip into the dark luxurious interior. It smells of leather and new car, and my heart is racing. Then it races even more as Rafael gets in beside me and the doors sweep gracefully down, enclosing us.

Georgios comes into the parking area just as we pull away from the kerb, and I can't help but give him a jaunty wave, thrilled with myself for having outwitted him. He'll come after me, of course—he knows where I'm going and he'll track my phone anyway—but for now, for the first time in my life, I'm on my own with a strange man.

Rafael drives with supreme confidence, manoeuvring through the traffic with ease, the car sliding in and out of lanes as if it's on rails.

'Oh my God,' I breathe, unable to contain my excitement. 'This is such a beautiful car.'

'It's a McLaren,' he says as we drive across a bridge. 'Handles beautifully.'

'So you like cars as well as driving them?'

'Yes.' He glances at me, onyx eyes glittering. 'That's three things you know about me now.'

I laugh, exhilaration swamping me. 'I feel bad. You know only one thing about me.'

'This is true. Which means you now owe me two facts about you.'

'Hmmm.' I make a show of thinking hard about what to say. 'I like Singapore, how's that?'

'That's one. I still need one more.'

'I'm going to have to think about that.' I give him a sidelong glance. His gaze is on the traffic in front of us, his large hands gripping the wheel with an easy mastery, and I can't stop studying his profile. I can't stop wondering about him and where he came from and why he affects me so powerfully.

The journey isn't long enough and to my disappointment we pull into Raffles far before I'm ready. The valet instantly appears as Rafael stops the car and we both get out. Then we're ushered into the hotel by the doorman.

Inside, the hotel is ornate and gilded and beautiful, and I feel Rafael's hand settle lightly in the small of my back. His palm is warm and the heat of it soaks through the silk and into my skin, making goosebumps rise all over me.

I haven't been touched by a man other than Ulysses since I was ten years old and so I'm acutely conscious of it. It feels different from when I grabbed his hand, because that was me touching him. Now he's touching me and I feel…breathless. As if every inch of my skin has been numb and I hadn't realised it, and now the numbness is fading, sending prickles of heat and sensation everywhere, like pins and needles.

I still can't think of anything else as we enter the historic Long Bar.

It's a shady space with floors of black and white tile, while the bar itself is all dark wood. Fans make the air cool and, while there are lots of people around, Rafael somehow manages to find us a cosy spot down one end of the bar.

His hand slips away as I perch on my bar stool, yet the warmth of his palm lingers on my skin. It makes my breath catch and my heart beat fast, adrenaline pumping hard through my veins. A part of me still can't believe I'm sitting here, in a bar in Singapore with a strange man, and neither my brother nor any of his staff are present. It's a miracle.

Rafael has ordered us both drinks and he sits with casual ease on his stool, his gaze burning into mine the way it did at the gala. It wants something from me, that gaze, something I can't name and yet want to give him all the same.

Our drinks arrive and mine is pink with a straw and a big slice of pineapple on the rim of the glass. Rafael watches me as I take a sip. 'Okay,' I say. 'The third thing you should know about me is that I like Singapore Slings.'

I'm expecting him to smile, but he doesn't and I can't stop the small dart of disappointment that goes through me. 'What's wrong?' I ask before I think better of it.

He is silent so long I don't think he's going to answer, but finally he says, 'You really shouldn't have come with me tonight, dragonfly.'

'Why not?' I ask. 'I mean, you really shouldn't have come with me considering I might be a serial killer of serial killers.'

Again, he doesn't smile. 'My intentions are not pure.'

A shiver goes right through me, tightening my skin. I'm sheltered, yes, but I'm not as innocent as he seems to think. I've known violence and pain, and I know what men are capable of.

'Maybe mine aren't pure, either.' I take another sip

of my drink. It's cold and delicious and tastes like a tropical night.

'Olympia,' he murmurs, making a poem out of my name.

Some part of me knows what he's talking about and I can't pretend that I don't. I can feel the electricity moving over my body when he looks at me, when his fingers touch mine, when our eyes meet. I can feel the tension.

Sexual tension.

'What do you want?' I ask and not because I don't know, but because I want him to say it. So I know that it's not just me who's feeling this pull between us.

'You,' he says, the dark intensity in his voice matched only by the dark intensity in his eyes. 'I knew from the moment I saw you.'

CHAPTER THREE

Rafael

Olympia's amber eyes widen as I give her the truth I hadn't meant to say tonight. No, tonight was supposed to be about connection, that's all. I intended to make the introductions and ease her into conversation, whet her appetite for me and make her hungry for more. I was *not* supposed to tell her I want her within the first hour of meeting her.

But she's nothing like I expected and everything I didn't know I wanted.

She's perched on the bar stool, her red lips wrapped around the straw in her glass, and she has no idea how impossibly sexy she is right now. She has no idea that what I'm thinking about is her mouth wrapped around my cock, leaving that pretty red lipstick on my skin.

I'm a rough man. Unsophisticated and unrefined, and this woman sitting on the stool is the very opposite. She's delicately beautiful, intensely feminine, and yet the glitter in her amber eyes hints at a passion locked away. A passion that would burn me alive if I wanted it to. And I want it to.

Except my revenge plan is a series of measured meetings, of her slowly but surely falling for me, not a headlong tumble into lust. And even if it were, the person who should be falling is her, not me.

Still, that lust can certainly be used to cement an obsession, so why not use it? I have no time for second thoughts, not when the opportunity is sitting right in front of me, so unguarded and open, with a hint of innocent wickedness that I find unbelievably tempting. The women I'm used to know the score with me and there's never conversation. Never flirtation. Only sex, hard and rough the way I like it.

None of them ever treat me the way Olympia's treating me now, as if we're old friends, taking my hand and teasing me, smiling at me so brightly it's almost impossible to look at her.

As we drove over the bridge in my car, I could barely keep my eyes on the road, distracted by the expression of absolute wonder on her face.

I'd only bought the McLaren the day before—my love of super cars is a vice I indulge in from time to time—and I'd found myself ridiculously pleased to take her for a drive in it.

I touched her when we arrived at the hotel, unable to help myself, because I could see the glances cast by various men as we got out of the car. They were all looking at her, drawn to her as I'd been drawn to her, so I put a possessive hand at the small of her back to show them she was mine. She didn't pull away, her skin so warm beneath my palm.

Somehow I managed to take my hand away in the

bar, though it was far more difficult than it should have been, and now all I can think about is how long it's been since I was with anyone who looked at the world the way she does. With awe and wonder. As if there are nothing but good things waiting out there and not monsters ready to tear you into pieces.

She's looking at me now as if I'm one of those good things, and the whispers of my long-dead conscience are telling me that using her to take my revenge is wrong. But they're only whispers and so I ignore them. She is a hibiscus in full bloom, all brilliant colour and unknowing passion, while I am the cold hand that will crush her, and I am okay with that.

She's blushing and yet she doesn't look away. 'You say it like that's a bad thing.'

'It is a bad thing.' A good man would have told her everything about his plans for revenge, and how he was going to use her. But I am not a good man. 'It's not what Georgios would want, I'm sure.'

She tilts her head, a hint of a smile curving her mouth. 'Fuck Georgios though, right?'

Her conscious imitation of me earlier and that smile are inviting me to smile back, but I don't. 'It's not what your brother would want, either.'

'I don't care about him.' She is looking at me steadily. 'What about if…if I wanted you too?'

The honesty of the question and that slight hesitation send a shock of heat through me, my muscles tensing, my cock hardening. It would be so easy to take her upstairs, to the suite I'm staying in, and lay her out across the big four-poster bed. Unwrap her like the gift she is.

Take my time enjoying her body, see what makes her gasp, what makes her moan, what makes her scream my name. I have scarves with me, soft ones that I could tie around her wrists to hold her gently while I set her passion burning, then make it explode as I—

No. I can't let myself get distracted by the sex when the sex is *not* the goal. Teaching her brother a fucking lesson is the goal. Taking everything away from him the way he took everything away from me is the goal.

I don't answer her. Instead I say, as a test, 'I should give you back to Georgios when you've finished your drink.'

Unexpectedly, small golden sparks light her eyes. 'No one "gives" me back to anyone,' she says, a hint of steel in her tone. 'I'm not an object.'

This small glimpse of anger is just as intoxicating as her wonder. Good. She's a woman of spirit, and I love a woman who can stand up for herself, who gives as good as she gets. My brain won't stop thinking about what that would look like in bed, no matter how much I tell myself that sex is not the goal.

'Of course you're not,' I say. 'But I'm sure you don't actually want me to take you up to my suite and fuck your brains out.' I'm blunt and crude on purpose, and maybe subconsciously I'm hoping she'll recoil and run away. I don't know if I can be polite any more. My meagre store of civil conversation was all used up at the gala and now this relentless attraction has eroded the rest of it, along with my patience, too. There is nothing left of me but crudity and rough stone in the vague shape of a man.

Her eyes widen slightly, but she doesn't recoil or run, which is unfortunate. Instead, something glows in the depths of her eyes. 'You're trying to frighten me away, aren't you?'

'Perhaps.' I've got nothing but honesty now. 'And perhaps you should be frightened, dragonfly.'

But she only shakes her head and before I can stop her, she reaches out and grabs my hand once more. Her slender fingers weave through mine, the heat of her skin a drug I can't get enough of. Once again, she's caught me, holding me still as surely as iron shackles would.

'I'm a virgin,' she says very clearly and without hesitation. 'I have never even kissed a man. For the past fifteen years of my life, I've been coddled and cosseted and protected like a child. But I'm not a child, Rafael.' My name on her lips... *Dio*. 'I came to Singapore to get away from Greece, to get away from my brother, to experience life without being slowly suffocated by all the cotton wool surrounding me.' Her hand in mine tightens, the expression in her amber eyes flaring. 'I've had my drink at Raffles Hotel and now I want more. I want you. I want to go up to your suite and I want you to show me what "fucking my brains out" means.'

That's the opposite of what you should be doing. Especially with a virgin like her.

But I ignore the thought. All I can see is the glow in her eyes and the burgeoning heat and, in this moment, even my fury at her brother is forgotten.

My hand tightens around hers and slowly, wordlessly, I pull her from the bar stool. She comes without hesitation and we leave the bar, me leading her up the wide stairs and corridors to one of the two Presidential Suites.

Inside, the room is dim and discreetly lit, and I'm so hungry and hard I want to take her immediately. But she is nervous, I can see it in the slight shake of her fingers as I let her go, so I restrain myself. 'Would you like something to drink?' I offer, trying to be gallant.

She glances around the opulence of the suite, to the luxurious couches gathered around a marble coffee table, and the long wall of high windows, the curtains now drawn, the chandeliers that hang from the ceiling. 'I'm not sure,' she says and then looks at me. 'I'm sorry. I'm a little…nervous.'

Now. Send her away now.

I should, but there will be no more second-guessing. My decision is made. So, I move over to her and look down into her lovely eyes. She gazes back at me, her expression open, hiding nothing. 'I think you should kiss me,' she says. 'That might help.'

Again, her painful honesty catches me hard, and I lift my hands, cupping her face between them. Her skin is warm against my palms and I leash the hungry beast in me, though it's far too late to cage it. She coaxed it out, fed it crumbs, and now it wants a whole meal.

'I won't hurt you,' I murmur, letting her see the truth as I hold her gaze. 'But I can't promise to be gentle either.' I want to tell her it's been a long time since I've had a woman, but it's not. Yet at the same time it feels as if it's been centuries.

She doesn't flinch or recoil. 'I don't need gentleness,' she says, her voice husky. 'I'm nervous, but I'm not made of china.'

No, she is not. She is warm and she smells like roses after rain, and her eyes are so brilliant I want to fall into them.

So I bend my head and my mouth brushes hers, gentle at first, to get her used to the sensation and to me. Her lips are petal soft and I hear her breath catch, and I wait a moment, trying to hold back the urge to gorge and to feast, letting her adjust. Then I kiss her again, light and easy, and this time I touch her lips with my tongue, coaxing her to open to me, and she does. Her mouth is warm too and she tastes of the sweetness of her cocktail, and I can't help but explore her more fully, more deeply.

A moan escapes her, her hands abruptly gripping my jacket, her body pressing itself delicately against mine, and then she is kissing me back, hesitant at first and shy, but growing bolder, her tongue exploring me in return.

My hold on my better self is failing, slipping out of my grip as she kisses me, the heat between us building. I slide a hand behind her, finding the zip of her scarlet silk dress and tugging it down. I want her naked and now, and I won't take no for an answer.

But she doesn't protest. She gives an impatient wriggle as the silk slides away from her, then she steps out of it still holding onto me, still trying to kiss me. She's wrestling with the buttons of my shirt, but I bat her hands away and tug at the thin silk of her scarlet bra until the straps break and I get rid of it.

I'm hungry now, starving in a way I've never been before. She's so fucking beautiful, I can't stand it, and I can't wait either.

I pull her down onto the carpet, naked but for a scrap of red silk hiding her sex and her high-heeled red sandals. I place a hand beside her head and lean over her, looking down into her golden eyes. They're blazing, her mouth full and red, and I can't tear my gaze away as I run a hand down her silky warm body, cupping one full breast and pinching her nipple, before going further, down between her pretty thighs, beneath the red silk, finding soft, wet folds and her hard little clit.

Her eyes widen as I touch her and she gasps as I stroke her. She's so wet and it's all for me, *because* of me. Her hips lift as I slide a finger inside her and she moans, her face flushed, white teeth sinking into her full bottom lip. I'm the first man to make her feel this way and the thought makes me savage. I never thought I was particularly possessive but now I've had my hands on her, I can't stand the thought of anyone else touching her.

I slide my fingers in and out of her, watching her writhe beneath me. She's close to a climax, I can tell, but not like this. I want to taste her. I want to eat her alive.

I remove my hand.

'No,' she whispers. 'Don't stop.'

'I'm not,' I tell her, then I tear her knickers off and spread her legs wide.

CHAPTER FOUR

Olympia

I'M SHAKING, WOUND SO tight I'm a clock spring about to snap. I didn't think it would happen so fast, that one minute he was kissing me, the next I'm naked and on my back on the carpet, Rafael Santangelo's large hands settling on my inner thighs and pressing them apart.

I didn't think my first time with a man would be so intense or so sudden, but down in the bar, when he told me he was going to give me back to Georgios like I was an unwanted gift, all I thought was *hell no*.

He told me he wanted me then tried to frighten me by telling me he was going to 'fuck my brains out', but he didn't know that I'm not a woman easily frightened by anything, let alone strong language.

What I am is a woman tired of being told what's best for her by men, and certainly what was best for me in that moment was him. I didn't expect to lose my virginity in Singapore, but I knew if I didn't insist on him taking me up to his suite, I was never going to lose it. Not with my brother watching my every move.

And anyway, when would I ever get the chance to

lose it to a man like this one? Dark and dangerous and so insanely attractive it hurts. Never, that's when, and never is too far away for me.

Yes, I was nervous when we got to his suite, but when he kissed me all of that fell away. I was dry tinder to a lit match and I went up in flames, the heat of his mouth and the touch of his tongue igniting a conflagration inside me that I had no hope of putting out. Not that I wanted to put it out.

His body was so hard and so hot, and I wanted him to burn with me. I wanted to touch him, feel his bare skin against mine, taste him. He smelled of a forest on a hot summer day, warm and spicy, and I wanted to bury my face in his neck and inhale him.

But he's leaving me with no chance to do that as he presses my legs apart, opening me up, and the way he's holding them wide makes my breath catch hard in my throat. He's looking down between my thighs and I feel my face burn with embarrassment even as excitement gathers in a tight hard knot.

Slowly, he slides a hand beneath each of my thighs and hooks my knees over his shoulders, his hands spreading me as he bends. His fingers are careful, but his gaze is ferocious as it meets mine. I'm panting, shivering all over, pleasure drawn to screaming point.

Then his head dips and I cry out as his tongue spears through the folds of my sex, exploring and hungry. I jerk again as he circles my clit and I can't stop the cries he brings from me. My hips lift to his mouth and when he puts his hands firmly on my hips, holding me down, I whimper.

'What do you want, dragonfly?' he whispers against my wet flesh. 'Tell me.'

'Y-you,' I stammer, finding it hard to get the words out. 'I want you.'

'You want me to what?' He gives me a long, slow lick as if I'm an ice cream melting in the sun. 'Be specific.'

I know what he wants me to say so I say it. 'I want y-you to make me c-come.'

'With my tongue or my fingers?'

I look down to where his dark head is between my thighs. I'm wearing my red sandals and nothing else, the heels digging into his back, and the sight is the most erotic thing I've ever seen. 'Y-your tongue,' I say shakily.

His head dips again and he pushes his tongue deep inside me, and I come apart and shatter like glass under pressure, pleasure exploding through every nerve ending and tearing a scream from my throat.

I lie there, dazed and shaking as he releases his hold on my thighs and moves away. Then I hear the sound of his fly being unzipped and he's back again, stretched above me, his hips between my thighs, one hand sliding beneath me, lifting me as the blunt head of his cock pushes into me.

He goes slowly, but I'm so wet there's no friction and no pain. I'm shaking as he gathers me close, easing deeper as I stretch around him, holding him as he holds me. It's a strange feeling, not bad, and yet not quite good either.

'Are you okay?' he asks roughly.

I manage a whisper. 'Y-yes.'

'Breathe, dragonfly,' he murmurs, watching me.

So I do and he begins to move and, like magic, the feeling of panic disappears, pleasure taking its place. It's good now, very good, very, *very* good and I'm trembling all over as I feel another orgasm begin to build.

'Better?' he asks, his dark eyes pinned to mine.

'Yes,' I breathe. 'Oh…my God, yes…'

He slides one large hand beneath my right thigh and lifts it up around his hips, enabling him to slide deeper, then he moves faster, harder. I groan, turning my face against the warmth of his neck, inhaling his scent as I press my eyes shut.

He's holding me so close, one hand gripping my thigh, the other cupping the back of my head, and even though he said he couldn't promise me gentleness, I sense he's trying to be gentle all the same.

I want to tell him that I meant it when I said I didn't need it, but I was wrong as it turned out. I don't know why this is shattering me, why his touch and the way he holds me is ripping me open, yet it is. I can't look him in the eye as we move together, it feels too intimate, too raw, and for the first time tonight, I'm feeling too vulnerable.

He moves even harder, faster, and then his fingers curl in my hair as he pulls my head back, and he's looking down at me, black eyes full of that ferocious heat, then he's kissing me, and it's not gentle at all. It's hard and it's savage and it's demanding, and when he lets go of my thigh, and slides a hand between us, his finger pressing down on my clit, I scream against his mouth as the climax takes me.

Even then he doesn't let me go, holding me fast as he chases his own orgasm, his teeth against my bottom lip as he finds it, his kiss a dark storm that sweeps me away.

A stillness settles over us afterwards and for a long moment I lie there on the carpet, his body a hot weight on mine. He's heavy, but I don't move. The wool of his trousers prickles against the soft skin of my inner thighs and the buttons of his half-undone shirt press against my tender breasts. His head is turned into my hair, his breath warm against the side of my neck.

I feel changed, as if the woman who entered this suite is not the same as the one who's lying on her back now, with her lover sprawled on top of her. And I don't know what to do. I should feel powerful and strong, perhaps, since I took matters into my own hands and did exactly what I wanted with the man I wanted it with. But I don't feel powerful or strong. I feel as if I've given away a vital part of myself to Rafael Santangelo and it's a part I'll never get back.

He moves finally, letting go my hair and raising his head, looking down at me. His dark eyes are searching. 'Did I hurt you?' he asks, his voice rusty-sounding.

'No.' My own voice doesn't sound much better. 'No, you didn't.'

He stares at me for a long moment and what he sees in my face I don't know, but suddenly he turns away, shifting off me. 'Georgios will be wondering where you are.' He gets to his feet and adjusts his clothing. He's very carefully not looking at me.

I sit up, confused and obscurely hurt though I don't know why. 'I already told you that I don't care about him.'

He bends to pick up my discarded dress. 'But your brother does.'

'Again, I already told you that I don't care about him either.' I get to my feet, conscious that, not only am I completely naked, my emotions are all over the place and I feel weird.

Rafael comes over to where I'm standing, my dress in his hands, and makes as if to cover me with it. I jerk back, staring up at him. His face is utterly expressionless, and the heat has disappeared from his dark eyes. In this moment he's never looked more like a stranger, not even when he was one. 'So that's it?' I ask, not knowing what I'm even asking for. 'We have sex and then you kick me out?'

'I don't have anything more to give you, Olympia.' His expression doesn't change. 'And yes, that's all I wanted.'

It feels as if he's slid a needle into my side, a small, sharp splinter of pain. 'But—'

'But what?' His voice is cold. 'Your brother is a powerful man. He's not an enemy I want.'

'What's my brother got to do with this?' I demand, inexplicable hurt radiating out like cracks in a mirror, jagged and sharp. 'This is about you and me.'

'No,' he corrects gently. 'It's just about you.'

My eyes prickle with unexpected tears, which makes

me abruptly furious. I was supposed to be stronger than this. I was supposed to be better. I was supposed to be able to handle anything the world could throw at me, and yet all it took for me to crumble was first-time sex with a strange man.

I snatch my dress from his fingers and turn away, angrily blinking back my tears, determined to hide them from him so he will never know how much this has hurt me. And it has hurt me. I am letting it matter, attaching some importance to it that it shouldn't have, and he's right. That's about me, not him.

He's silent behind me as I pull on my dress and I don't turn back once it's done. I don't look over my shoulder at all as I stride on shaky legs to the door of the suite.

'Dragonfly,' he says softly. 'Wait.'

But I don't.

I pull open the door and walk through it without a backward glance.

CHAPTER FIVE

Rafael

IT'S CHRISTMAS EVE and I'm sitting in a plain black car parked in one of Athens' narrow back streets near the Acropolis. I have a jewelled hair clip in one hand and it glitters in the cold light that comes through the windows, all blue and red and gold. A dragonfly. A souvenir from that night in Singapore nearly four months ago and from the woman who turned my revenge plans upside down.

I shouldn't have kept it, but I felt I deserved something for the sacrifice I made when I made sure she left me without looking back. Despite all my good intentions to use lust to cement an obsession with me, in the end it was I who was in danger of becoming obsessed. And I couldn't allow that to happen. I couldn't even allow the possibility in case it distracted me from my ultimate goal of breaking her bastard of a brother. So instead I made sure she walked away from me and stayed away.

Except nothing turns out the way you expect.

She'll be coming soon—my driver is tracking her

phone—and she's close by. I called her this morning, asking her to meet and, after she'd got over her shock at hearing from me, she agreed. I didn't tell her why I needed to see her, and she didn't ask, but we both knew the reason.

There were consequences from our night in Singapore, consequences that I had confirmation of only a couple of days ago. I should have thought that night, should have been more aware, but she managed to make me so hungry that the thought of protection didn't even cross my mind.

It has been nagging at the back of my brain for weeks, the sense that I missed something, that something isn't quite right, yet it wasn't till a couple of months had passed that I'd woken in the middle of the night with the answer front and centre in my head. No condom.

The first thing I did the next day was to attempt to contact her or someone close to her, but she'd retreated from the world again, back into her brother's house and protected by his security. She might as well have been on the moon, that's how unreachable she was to me.

But I've never been one to give up, so, after months of enquiries and bribes being exchanged for the information, I learned that she'd been to see a doctor recently, and not her usual one. Alarm bells were already ringing by the time I finally tracked that doctor down, and again, money talked—the good doctor had debts to pay—and I received the confirmation I'd been dreading.

My dragonfly is pregnant and the child is mine.

I'd sent her away that night to keep my own goal pure, to formulate new plans that didn't include her, but now...

Things are different now. Even though I'm no decent father for a child, I can't abandon one I helped bring into the world.

Don't lie. You know what you really want.

I stare at the jewelled hair clip in my hand.

It's true. If I really was a decent father, I wouldn't be here. I'd be providing Olympia with money should she need it, but I certainly wouldn't be waiting for her to show, yet again with intentions far from pure.

The real truth is that I'm not a good man and this pregnancy has just handed my revenge to me on a golden platter and it's too good an opportunity to refuse.

Ulysses Zakynthos is a famous bachelor. A famous *childless* bachelor, which makes Olympia his heir. It will also make *my* child his heir, and if I marry her, then what is hers is also mine and that includes Vulcan Energy.

I've spent the past couple of months congratulating myself for seeing the trap she could end up being for me and so sending her away. But when the confirmation of her pregnancy came through, it seemed as if fate had had a hand in my future after all.

The fact that she's expecting my child has changed everything. And I'm not a good man, not even slightly. I'm still what I am, a man ruthless in pursuit of his goal, and so I will claim her, I will claim my child, and then I will claim Vulcan Energy, and once I have, I'll have taken everything Ulysses Zakynthos holds dear.

Only then will my parents have justice. Only then will they have peace. And nothing is more important than that. Nothing.

'She's coming,' my driver informs me.

I lift my head and stare out the window of the car.

There's a taverna across the street and I sent her instructions to meet me there, and, despite the chill, there are crowds coming and going through its doors, celebrating Christmas Eve. A small figure is weaving around the crowds and I know immediately it's her. The only reason she's managed to escape her brother's house is because he's not here. He's in LA, arriving tomorrow, or at least that's what the flight plan for his private jet said, and that's good. That has granted me time to make my own plans.

He has no idea that his world is about to come crashing down on him, because I am going to take Olympia back to my home in Sicily and I do not intend to set her free again.

As she makes her way towards the car, I take a few moments to watch her, to see if she's the same as she was four months ago and if my reaction to her is the same too. In my mind I've tried to minimise it, tried to explain it away. It was sexual tension, nothing more, and I've had the same with many women.

Then again, I've never been so hungry for one woman that I forgot a condom, or been haunted by her for weeks on end, not as I have with Olympia. I tried to spend a night with one of my more regular lovers not long after I returned from Singapore, but the thought didn't excite me. I only went through the motions, determined to scrub Olympia from my mind, and I failed. Failed utterly.

Now she's coming closer and the blood in my veins starts to pump hard, my heartbeat accelerating. I want her. I want her now, here, in the back of the car, with her legs spread wide and her high heels digging into my spine. I want her panting in my ear, before screaming my name as I taste her. I want to bind her hands and her ankles, using restraint to heighten every stroke and every lick, every kiss that I give her…

She's just about through the crowd and preparing to cross the street, when a man lumbers down the steps of the taverna and nearly knocks her off her feet.

Instantly, I throw open the door and leap out of the car, striding across the street, my black overcoat flaring out behind me. The crowd around the taverna entrance is noisy but they fall silent as I approach.

The man who nearly knocked her over doesn't see me, he's too busy apologising to her, but she sees me. Her amber eyes flame as they meet mine and once again I feel it, that arrow that hits me dead centre of my chest.

Her black hair is loose over her shoulders and she's wearing a soft-looking red coat, and all I can think is that she should always wear red. I'll marry her in a red gown, make sure her wardrobe is full of red, and when she kneels before me, she'll be wearing red lipstick.

The man, sensing the silence that has followed me,

turns quickly, spots me and my taut expression, and pales. 'I'm sorry, I didn't see—'

I hold up a hand and he breaks off. I don't speak. I merely go to where Olympia is standing and I slide my arm around her waist, drawing her into my side. Then, holding her close, I escort her back to the car.

She holds herself rigid, as if she's only suffering my arm around her, but she doesn't protest. It's only as we get to the car that she pulls away abruptly. 'What do you want, Rafael?' she asks, her voice flat.

The lights shine on her lovely face, her eyes like liquid gold. She smiled at me four months ago, like the sun coming out from behind a cloud, but there are no smiles for me tonight, no sparks of mischief in her gaze. She looks pale, and there are shadows under her eyes.

My chest tightens inexplicably. 'It's too cold to stand here,' I say. 'Get in the car.'

'No.' She folds her arms, the look on her face implacable. 'You called me saying that we needed to talk. So. What do you want to talk about?'

She must know why I'm here—why else would I have wanted to meet? Then again, maybe she doesn't. Maybe she's expecting me to ask her for another night together. What is very clear is that she doesn't want me to know she's pregnant.

Her brother will be in the air by now and, while it takes hours to get from LA to Athens, I can't afford to spend too much time here. I need to be back in Sicily before he arrives.

'Please,' I say, trying for patience and not to let my

roiling emotions leak into my voice. 'Get in the car, dragonfly.'

She blinks at the name and her perfect mouth goes soft. But then she takes a step back. 'No, no. You can't just come back here acting as if—'

'I know you're pregnant,' I interrupt, my remaining patience abruptly slipping. 'Four months, to be exact, which makes me the father of your child. So, I'll ask again. Get in the car or I will put you in it.'

She pales at my tone, yet her chin juts mutinously. I remember that steel in her. I only caught a glimpse of it four months ago, but it's on full display now.

I think she's not going to do it and I don't want to have to carry out my threat, but I will if I have to. Then she lets out an angry breath and gets into the back seat of the car. I slide in beside her, shut the door, and give my driver the okay to go.

'Wait.' Olympia looks around a little wildly as the car pulls into the street. 'Where are we going?' This time when her eyes meet mine, they're full of golden sparks. 'What are you doing, Rafael? I thought we were just going to talk.'

I sit back in the seat next to her. 'We will. When we get to my home in Sicily.'

'What?' She stares at me in shock. 'I'm not going to Sicily with you. Are you completely mad?'

'No.' I turn to look at her, pinning her with my gaze. 'Why didn't you tell me about the pregnancy?'

Sparks glitter in her eyes for a moment, then she looks away out the window of the car as we weave through the traffic and the back streets, heading towards the motorway that will take us out of the city to the airport where my jet is ready to leave. Her hands twist in her lap. I want to pull aside her coat, see the swell of her belly where my child lies. Cold confirmation by phone is one thing, but I want to see the evidence for myself.

'Stop the car,' she says. 'Let me out.'

I reach for her chin, gripping it and turning her face towards me. 'Answer the question, Olympia. You owe me that at least.'

Her gaze is furious, but she makes no move to pull away. 'I haven't told anyone, if you must know. Not even my brother.'

Protective rage presses against my throat. 'Why not? Will he hurt you? Did he do—?'

'Of course not.' She jerks her chin out of my grip. 'Why the hell would you think that?'

I shouldn't be talking about her brother. I'm not supposed to know anything about him or how he keeps her, yet anger and a powerful, inexplicable jealousy are choking me. 'He keeps you a prisoner, doesn't he?' I demand. 'Were you afraid to tell him? Is that why you didn't?' I'm crossing my own self-imposed boundaries and yet I can't seem to stop. 'Were you afraid he'd hurt our child?'

Her eyes widen, shock flickering through the amber depths. She says nothing, staring blankly at me, but I can see her brain working furiously behind her eyes. This woman might have complained about her idiocy four months ago, but there is nothing idiotic about her, nothing at all.

'What do you mean he keeps me prisoner?' she asks.

Goddamn. She's going to guess my motives and I know it. So much for her being sheltered and, by her own admission, coddled and cosseted. That might be true, but it doesn't mean she's not smart. In fact, I would hazard a guess that she's far too smart for her own good and most certainly for mine.

'The rumours,' I say, attempting to be dismissive. 'You've never been seen out of the house and you're never photographed anywhere. People talk.'

She stares at me as if she's never seen me before in her entire life. 'Who are you?' There's a trace of panic in her voice. 'What do you want?'

I don't want to scare her, that's the last thing I want to do, but she keeps seeing more than I want her to. She can sense there's more to me than a man she slept with once four months ago.

My muscles are rigid, my hands wanting to reach across the gap between us and pull her close, silence her and her questions with my mouth. I don't understand why I'm so reluctant to tell her the truth. What does it matter if she knows? She can't run from me, not now I have her. Do I really care about how she sees me? It doesn't matter now surely?

I meet her gaze. 'You know who I am, dragonfly. I'm Rafael Santangelo. I own Atlas Construction. And now I own you.'

CHAPTER SIX

Olympia

PANIC THREATENS, BUT I push it away as I stare at the man sitting bare inches from me. He's all in black and when he appeared outside the taverna, striding towards me after I was nearly knocked over by some drunken idiot, he seemed like some evil force out of a fantasy novel with his black coat flaring out behind him. A storm crow or Dracula ready to claim a victim.

Rafael Santangelo. The man I lost my virginity to four months ago in Singapore. The father of my child.

My mouth is dry as the desert, my heartbeat racing.

When I got his call a couple of hours ago, I was shocked to the core. Back in Singapore, his unrestrained passion, the hunger he had for me made me feel stronger than I had in years. Only for all of that to then break apart when he sent me away. I didn't want to feel broken afterwards—he was a stranger after all so why should I let him matter?—yet a part of me did. A part of me wondered if I was really as strong as I thought I was if a mere stranger could hurt me so badly.

But I wasn't going to give in to those doubts, not

after how I'd battled my way through the darkness of my past for so many years, and so I was determined to forget him, to chalk him up to experience. I refused to acknowledge that he'd hurt me. I refused to let him slide under my skin and stay there like the barb he was.

When I got back to Athens, I told Ulysses that I'd had a wonderful time, but I was happy to be home. He was pleased for me, but he didn't offer to let me represent him at any other social occasion and I didn't ask. I wanted to stay in my safe place, with the people I was familiar with, with the beach I loved at my doorstep, and where nothing could hurt me.

But, of course, no matter how much I refused to think of him, Rafael kept creeping into my thoughts and into my dreams, too. I dreamt of being in his arms, his black eyes looking down into mine, his deep, dark voice saying, 'Dragonfly...wait...' I'd wake up after those dreams hot and sweaty, my body aching and restless.

I hated it. So I busied myself with the online jewellery-making course I was taking, trying to lose myself in plans for the studio Ulysses promised he'd build for me, where I could indulge in all my little creative hobbies.

Then I started to feel tired, unusually so, and my sense of smell seemed more acute. My period, always irregular, just didn't turn up at all and my breasts hurt. I tried to ignore the symptoms as much as I could, because the possibility that kept nagging at me couldn't happen, it just couldn't.

But then, after I had to leave the dining room

abruptly to throw up when our housekeeper served a fish meal, as I sat on the bathroom floor, my stomach still acid and unsettled, I was forced to confront the possibility I'd been ignoring for at least a couple of months, and it scared me to death.

I had no idea what I was going to say to Ulysses, so I didn't say anything at all. I booked myself a doctor's appointment with a doctor who didn't know me or my brother, then sneaked out of the house, leaving my bodyguards none the wiser.

The doctor gave me the confirmation I'd been dreading and afterwards, I'd wandered around the city streets in a daze, feeling as if my entire world was collapsing.

I was pregnant to the man I'd met in Singapore, to Rafael Santangelo, and I didn't know what to do. I didn't know if I was going to keep the baby. I didn't know how to tell Ulysses that I'd betrayed the trust he'd put in me to keep myself safe. I didn't know how to contact Rafael or even what to say to him, and I was afraid, terribly, terribly afraid.

I was already three months along, the doctor said, and that made everything that much more difficult.

In the end, I'd gone home and tried not to think about it since hiding my head in the sand was what I did best. I wore looser clothes and pretended nothing was wrong, that I was completely and utterly fine, and Ulysses didn't suspect a thing.

I might have even convinced myself if I hadn't got a call from a strange number earlier this morning. I answered it unthinkingly and a familiar voice, dark and deep, spoke, saying that he was Rafael Santangelo and he wanted to meet, because we needed to talk. My mind had gone blank with shock so I made a note of the time and the place, and agreed to meet him.

It wasn't until afterwards that I had second thoughts, because while he hadn't said anything about the pregnancy, why else would he have called me? And did I really want to leave the safety of my house for a meeting with a relative stranger? Ulysses wouldn't have let me go, or at least not without my security, and for a couple of moments I toyed with the idea of just not going at all.

But I knew I couldn't. He was the father of the baby and, whether he knew already or not, I had to face him. Ulysses had been very good at solving my problems since the day he'd rescued me from my abusive foster parents, yet he couldn't solve this one. It was mine to deal with and deal with it I would.

So I'd dismissed my security—they made no argument since it was Christmas Eve and they wanted to spend time with their families—and went into the city.

I'd braced myself to see him, stoking my anger at how he'd left things between us because I needed it for the strength to face him. But seeing him has left that strength in ruins.

Now I'm sitting in the dim interior of this featureless black car, and I can't help the instinctive heat that blooms inside me as I inhale the warm forest spice of his scent, feel the dark, dense pressure of his gaze.

He's just as magnetic, just as compelling as he was four months ago, but now there's an…edge to his presence that wasn't there when I first met him. Or maybe it was and I just didn't notice. Anyway, I can feel that edge now and it's dangerous. It makes me afraid, yet the fear is also somehow laced through with excitement and an anticipation that I shouldn't feel.

I mean, the man is essentially kidnapping me, taking me away from the brother I could never bring myself to leave, so excited is the last thing I should be.

'You don't own me,' I snap, holding onto my anger for dear life. 'Don't be so damn arrogant.'

His onyx eyes glitter in the dark, though he remains silent.

I can't stop thinking of what he said about Ulysses keeping me a prisoner. Firstly, it's not true, I'm *not* a prisoner, even though sometimes I feel suffocated by my brother's overprotectiveness. And secondly, why does Rafael think that means I'm Ulysses's captive? He said something about a rumour, and I suppose that might be the case. Ulysses is in the media frequently, though he never talks about me.

And yet... Rafael said it so emphatically, his dark eyes searching my face. He even thought Ulysses would hurt me or the baby, which is ludicrous. My brother has a reputation for ruthlessness, it's true, but there's no way he'd hurt me, let alone his little niece or nephew, so why Rafael assumed he'd do so is inexplicable.

I stare at him and it occurs to me now that there is a lot that's inexplicable about this man. I know next to nothing about him, except that he owns Atlas Construction, which I've never heard of, and that he's Sicilian and he likes cars.

And he likes you, remember?

No, he doesn't like me. If he liked me, he wouldn't have forced me into his car and we wouldn't now be speeding towards the airport.

Panic claws at my throat at the thought of what will happen when Ulysses finds me gone, but I force it away. I will not let it get the better of me, I'm stronger than that. I used to get frequent nightmares after Ulysses rescued me, and I'd wake up with this same feeling of panic coiling like a snake in my gut. He would hold me, his strong arms around me reminding me that I was okay, that I was safe.

Gradually those nightmares got less and less frequent until at last they stopped, and I haven't had one in years. I haven't felt that same sick fear that used to incapacitate me in years either, and I won't let it take a hold of me now.

I'm not ten any more, hiding in the wardrobe of my brother's house, too scared to come out. I'm twenty-five and I'm stronger than I've ever been. I handled Rafael Santangelo back in Singapore, no matter what he broke when he sent me away, and I'll handle him now.

I swallow the fear using the tricks my therapist taught me, such as being conscious of where I am and the things around me. The leather of the seat I'm sitting on. The low purr of the car's engine. The flash of street lights making Rafael's eyes glitter. The hard, expressionless lines of his face…

'So, what exactly is the plan?' I force my voice to remain steady. 'You're going to take me to Sicily and then what? I need to call my brother and tell him where I am.'

'You can call him when we get there.'

'And after?'

'We're not having this conversation now,' he says flatly. 'I'll explain everything when we get there.'

'No.' I try my best to channel Ulysses, injecting as much command into the words as I can. 'You will explain now.'

Rafael says nothing, staring back at me as we engage in a silent battle of wills, the atmosphere in the car, already thick with tension, becoming even thicker, dense as a storm cloud.

His phone abruptly rings and he pulls it out of his pocket, glances at the screen, then answers it in a stream of liquid Italian. The sudden release of tension makes me gasp silently for air as he turns away, still talking.

It's very clear that he's not going to give me any explanations until he's ready and I know from experience that it's pointless to push with a man that stubborn. My brother is the same, not budging from whatever position he's taking, not until he's good and ready, which I've always found incredibly frustrating.

However, it's also been my experience that a stubborn man can be handled if you find his point of vulnerability and Ulysses's point of vulnerability is me and my happiness.

A pang of grief and worry hits me yet again at the thought of my brother and the empty house he'll come back to, but I push it aside, turning away instead as Rafael keeps on talking, staring sightlessly out at the cars flashing by on the motorway. Maybe Rafael is the same. Maybe he has a chink in his armour somewhere. Ulysses will generally do what I want if I make it about how happy it would make me, but I'm assuming Rafael won't care about my happiness, so I'll have to find another vulnerability.

I give him a sidelong glance. He's still talking, not paying any attention to me. His voice is implacable, the lines of his face hard, his mouth cruel. But that mouth wasn't cruel when it was on mine, and the lines of his face weren't hard when he was inside me. They were fierce with hunger and desperation.

Does he still want me? Could that be his weakness? I need to find out at some point, because I have to have something to right the balance of power in my favour.

You could use the baby.

Instinctively, I put a protective hand over the swell of my belly. No, that wouldn't be right, I would never use any child like that, let alone my own.

It's his as well, don't forget that.

As if I could, especially when he's made it so clear he has no intention of letting me forget it.

I remain silent for the rest of the trip to the airport. Rafael makes other phone calls, but since he's speaking Italian, which I don't understand, I have no idea who he's talking to or why.

Once we reach the airport, Rafael goes to deal with some officials, while I am escorted to a small private jet that sits on the runway, all ready to go. Once I'm belted into my seat, Rafael arrives and the plane door is shut. We take off almost immediately, leaving the lights of Athens and my home behind us.

It's a quick flight and in just a couple of hours we're already descending into Palermo. Rafael does not speak or at least not to me. He's still busy with his phone, either talking or typing on the screen.

As we disembark the plane, Rafael indicates that I should follow him to where a sleek red low-slung car waits. It's the same one he drove me to Raffles in, the doors opening like wings as he ushers me into it. He must *really* like cars if he had this shipped back to Sicily.

We leave the airport and Palermo behind us, and soon we're following narrow, twisting roads that wind along the rocky coastline, before curling inland again. Rafael is silent, making good on his determination to tell me nothing until we get to wherever we're going. It's frustrating, but protesting and making a fuss won't get me anywhere. I've learned patience over the years and, anyway, there is a tiny part of me that keeps whispering that I'm in Sicily and how wonderful to be out of Athens again, to be away from my bodyguards and my brother's overprotective security. At least, it would be wonderful if I wasn't in the hands of yet another man, seemingly hellbent on ordering me around and making me do whatever he wants.

Eventually, after an interminable trip in darkness, we turn onto a very narrow lane, with stone walls on either side, that twists once again in the direction of the coast. A driveway leads off it and Rafael follows it as it winds through tall pines before opening out into a wide gravel area in front of an ancient-looking villa built of stone.

I stare, open-mouthed. It's beautiful. The stone is pale grey, the sloped roofline covered in old terracotta tiles. There are colonnades and wide porticos, green lawns and rows of cypresses. Discreet garden lighting illuminates the old stone walls and giant terracotta pots full of herbs and other shrubs.

Rafael parks the car and the doors open. The air is cold, but I can smell the sea. It must be close, perhaps just beyond the cliffs that the villa backs onto.

I get out and he ushers me to the villa's front doors, opening them then standing aside to let me enter first. It's warm inside the house and it smells of pine, reminding me of home, and some of the tension in my muscles relaxes.

'Come,' Rafael says imperiously, gesturing at me. I follow him down a wide central hallway, the walls smooth and whitewashed, before we come to a long, airy lounge area. There are tall windows along one wall, the view obscured by the curtains that have been drawn. A fireplace is down one end, the leaping fire sending out heat into the room, and gathered around the fireplace are a group of soft-looking couches and armchairs. Bizarrely, or maybe not so bizarrely since it is Christmas Eve, a Christmas tree stands beside the fire decorated with glass baubles and tinsel.

My heart catches oddly at the sight. I love decorating our tree at home, because every Christmas Ulysses buys me a new ornament, and I love hanging them all up, a record of how many wonderful Christmases I've had to balance out all the ones I didn't.

Ulysses will be on his way with a new ornament for

me, but I won't be there. Our house will be dark and cold, and he'll be worried.

My throat closes as my concern for him returns. I hate to make my brother worried. It seems a poor reward for everything he's done for me.

Rafael indicates the couch near the fire. 'Sit,' he orders, his tone hard.

I don't move. 'I need to call Ulysses.'

'Not yet.' He stands in front of the fire, his arms folded, black eyes glittering. 'Sit.'

I don't want to, but again, fighting him on little things like being ordered around is futile and a waste of energy. I don't feel as tired as I did in the early days of the pregnancy, but I'm still tired, not to mention cold, and the thought of sitting before a warm fire is tempting.

So I lift my chin and walk unhurriedly over to the couch then sit down, wrapping my red coat around me. Rafael does not sit, keeping his position in front of the fire and staring down at me. He's very tall and very broad, and I remember the feel of his body against mine, the heat of his skin and the hard flex of his muscles. A powerful man and, right now, a dangerous one too.

My heart kicks against my ribs and I can't tell if it's with fear or excitement, or a heady combination of both.

'Well?' I demand, ignoring it. 'We're here. So. Talk.'

CHAPTER SEVEN

Rafael

SHE SITS ON the couch in front of me, wrapped in her red coat, her inky hair spilling over it. Her cheeks are flushed from the cool night air and her amber eyes are as bright with anger as the flames at my back. She has a reason to be angry, it's true, but I'm not going to let that deter me.

I spent the journey from Athens to my villa on the coast of Sicily organising everything I need to claim her once and for all. A marriage licence. A priest to conduct the ceremony. Rings and a gown for her, as well as an entirely new wardrobe of clothes suitable for a pregnant woman. Then, of course, a doctor to look after her pregnancy.

The villa is special to me. It's my family home, the place I was born in and grew up in, and it's the one thing I have of my parents that I managed to save from being sold after my father died. I had financial help to save it, naturally, and that help came with strings attached. Those *Cosa Nostra* strings, to be precise, and I was in no position to refuse. I did cut those strings eventually, but by then it was too late. The violence I meted out as an enforcer ended up tainting my soul and that taint will never come out.

Olympia will live here and our baby will be born here, too, and I will not be moved on this. She won't like it, I can already tell that the golden flames in her eyes will burn higher once she finds out, but I will brook no argument. It's the most secure of my residences, not to mention one that no one knows about, so if her brother comes looking for her—and he will, I have no doubt—he'll have to work at finding her.

'You're pregnant with my child,' I say into the heavy silence.

'Really? I had no idea.' Her tone is sarcastic, the look she gives me disdainful.

She looks so composed sitting there on the couch, as if she's isolating herself as much as possible from her surroundings and purposely. There is no sign of her beautiful smile, no glints of mischief in her eyes, none of the warm openness she treated me with back in Singapore.

Now, her chin is lifted and her expression is haughty almost, as if she is an empress and I am merely the lackey there to do her bidding, and not the man looking to bind her to him forever.

Brave, dragonfly.

'Why the fuck didn't you tell me?' I don't try to make the question sound any less than the demand it is or attempt to hide the fury lacing the words.

Her chin lifts a little higher in response. 'Because I didn't want to believe it was true. I tried not to think about it for the first few months and then, when I couldn't *not* think about it, I went to the doctor.' Her gaze turns challenging. 'And I think the more appropriate question is how do you know?'

She's trying to change the subject, but I won't be distracted. 'You tried not to think about it? And how long exactly were you planning on doing that?'

'I don't know,' she shoots back. 'It's not like I've ever been pregnant before.'

Don't harangue her. It's your child she's pregnant with and it's hardly her fault. She was a sheltered virgin, which means the responsibility for protection was on you.

It's an unwelcome thought. It's true that the duty for protection that night was mine, and one I failed at, and I don't like failing, not at anything. I also don't like the twist of sympathy tightening in my chest that has me noting the darkened shadows under her pretty eyes and thinking that perhaps tucking her up into bed is what I should be doing instead of having this conversation.

But it's a conversation we need to have and better to have it now than later, so I say, 'I'm not hard to find, Olympia. You should have contacted me.'

'Fine, I should have and I didn't. I'm sorry. Now, answer the question.'

This time I accept the distraction. 'How did I find out? It wasn't until after I left Singapore that I remembered we had used no protection. So I tried to find your contact details to get in touch with you, but I was unable to find any.' I pause. 'Your brother keeps you extremely well hidden.'

She ignores that, continuing to stare hostilely at me.

'I have contacts that can get me information for a price,' I go on. 'And I was able to find out which doctor you went to see, then I bribed her to tell me what it was about. She told me you were pregnant.'

Incredulity ripples over Olympia's face. 'You bribed her?'

She is horrified, as any normal law-abiding person would be. Then again, being horrified is a privilege, which she would most certainly have as the cosseted sister of a very rich and powerful man.

But I don't point that out, instead I say, 'It wasn't ideal but I needed to know, since it was clear you weren't going to tell me.'

She has the grace to look away at that, but it shows more clearly the faint, dark shadows beneath her eyes, and the wave of protectiveness hits me again, the urge to wrap her up and put her to sleep in my bed almost overwhelming me. But I resist. We need to have this conversation and we need to have it now.

'The baby is mine,' I say into the heavy silence. 'And I am going to claim it, Olympia. Which is why we will be getting married as soon as possible.'

Her head turns, her gaze snapping back to mine. 'What?'

'The child will have my name,' I say. 'It will be my heir and, for the greatest legal protection for both the baby and you, we need to marry.'

She blinks, obviously struggling to process what I've just said. 'But…but I don't want to marry you.'

'I don't care. You are marrying me and that is final.'

Her gaze flares and abruptly she pushes herself up off the couch, coming to stand right in front of me, all bright fury and challenge. 'Just because you're the father of my baby doesn't give you the right to tell me what to do. I am *not* marrying you, you stupid man. I am not marrying *anyone*.'

She's standing very close and I can smell the deliciously sweet scent of her, roses after rain, and she's warm, and instantly I'm so hard it's almost painful. It's inexplicable that I should feel this way, after all, I've already had her and it's not as if I've been a monk in the months since. I shouldn't be so hungry, so desperate, and yet my body isn't listening to sense and she's impossible to resist.

I can't stop myself from reaching out to grip her upper arms and I hear the rush of her indrawn breath as my fingers close on the soft wool of her coat. Her eyes widen and her mouth opens. Her lips are as full and red as her coat, and I remember how they taste. I remember how *she* tastes and once again... *Dio*.

She's breathing fast and, as I watch, her pupils dilate. She feels it too, I know she does. I can see it in her eyes, in the pulse that beats hard and fast at the base of her throat. I don't move and neither does she as our gazes lock and hold.

'You have been haunting me for four months, dragonfly,' I hear myself say in a rough voice, even though I never meant to speak. 'You need to stop.'

She takes a shaky breath. 'Why? It was clear you were done with me when you told me to leave.'

Beneath the fury in her amber eyes, I see the hurt.

I can hear it in her voice, too. I heard it that same night, just before she walked out the door, but that was because I wanted her to forget me. Yet it's clear she hasn't and, even though it's wrong, that pleases me. That pleases me *intensely*.

'I lied.' I should release her, yet my fingers tighten instead.

She doesn't seem to notice. Her amber gaze searches mine, searching for the truth. 'Why?'

I can't give her the truth. I can't tell her my real motivations, not at this delicate stage. The shock might hurt her and the baby, and for some reason I can't stand the thought of that, so I settle for a lesser truth. 'Because I am a bad man. And I thought it was better if you stayed away from me.'

'A bad man,' she echoes, her gaze dropping to my mouth and then back up again. Her breathing has accelerated, I can hear it. She's hungry. She's hungry just like me. 'I don't think you are.'

'You don't know me.' I can feel her heat, her luscious body so close to mine, and I can't think with her so close. I should step away. I can't afford to be distracted while we're discussing this and yet I can't make myself release her. 'You know nothing about me.'

Her hands are rising, fingers curling around the lapels of my coat, her gaze on mine hypnotic. 'But you know about me, don't you? You know my brother, too.'

The blood is pumping hard in my veins, the scent of her winding around me. She's going to guess my secret if I'm not careful and I can't have her doing that. I need to take control of this somehow and yet it feels impossible. The basest parts of me are now in command and I can't resist.

'Show me,' I grit out, releasing her arms to grip the edges of her coat instead. 'Show me what I did to you.'

She blinks, not understanding for a moment. Then she does, and colour riots over her face. 'I don't think—'

But I'm already pulling open her coat and glancing down. She's wearing a simple, stretchy black dress that moulds to her every curve, including the small rounded bump of her stomach. Where my child lies.

Possessiveness slides long fingers around my throat, choking me. The sight has turned me into the most basic version of myself, and I put out a hand to touch her, tracing that soft curve.

I never wanted a wife or children, even though my childhood was idyllic. But after my father died the child I once was would have been horrified at the things I did to survive. To work my way up the command chain until I owned the company I used to work for. To make it one of the biggest construction companies in Europe in a few short years. The people I dealt with, the sacrifices I made, the blind eyes I turned and all to get where I am today. Positioned perfectly to take Vulcan Energy out from under Ulysses Zakynthos's nose.

I'd make a terrible father and I know it, yet the fact that I will be one is staring me in the face and I can't walk away. I should, of course. Let her go and let my child go with her, and yet I'm not going to. I will keep them both, even if I have to destroy myself to do so.

She shivers as I lay a palm on her stomach and I meet her gaze. She's so warm, her pupils dilating as my fingers trace that beautiful curve. And I don't stop. I slide my hand down, cupping her stomach, watching the colour burn in her cheeks. Her mouth opens and a breath escapes her as I slide my hand down even further, down between her thighs and pressing gently through the fabric of her dress.

Her fingers grip the lapels of my coat tightly, her breathing getting faster as I press harder. 'Rafael…' she whispers, her gaze still pinned to mine.

I can see desperation there and rising flames, and so I don't stop. I stroke her through her dress, listening to her breathing get even faster, watching pleasure suffuse her beautiful face.

She's trembling so I slide my other arm around her waist, pulling her close, supporting her as I stroke, finding her clit and circling softly, gently. She gasps and begins to pant, her knuckles white as she grips my coat, pleasure turning her inside out.

I'm rock hard, my body screaming at me to end this with her on her back, but I don't want to stop, I don't want her to let me go. I want to watch her come, listen to her gasp my name again and so I don't stop. I stroke and circle with my fingers, until her body stiffens in my hold and she's shaking, and then I bend my head, covering her mouth with mine as she comes.

CHAPTER EIGHT

Olympia

I'M SHIVERING AGAINST him as the aftershocks hit me. His arm is like iron around my waist and I'm gripping his coat for dear life. His mouth is gentle though, in stark contrast to the agonising pleasure that ripped me apart. I can't do anything but hold on as the sweetness of his kiss devastates me.

I don't know what happened. One moment I was sitting on the couch while he stood over me, tall and dark and dangerous, telling me I had to marry him. Next minute, I was up against him, gripping his coat, lost as a storm of desire took me, the heat of his body and the delicious scent of his aftershave, the one that's been haunting my dreams for months, freezing me in place.

He looked down at me, some storm of emotion I couldn't untangle flickering in his dark eyes as I'd demanded to know why he'd sent me away that night in Singapore. I shouldn't have betrayed that it mattered to me, but I hadn't been able to mask my hurt. And then he'd told me he'd lied, that he hadn't been done with me at all, and through my shock had come triumph.

He'd felt it too, this...*thing* between us, still burning and still burning hot.

A bad man, that's what he is, he said, and I told him he was wrong. Because how could a bad man make me feel this way? Make me feel as if I'd die if he didn't touch me. And then he'd ripped open my coat, his gaze on my stomach and there had been a feral light in his eyes as he'd touched me.

I hadn't been able to look away from his face, shivers wracking me as his hand followed the curve of my stomach and then down further. I should have pushed myself away, but I couldn't do it. His touch felt too good, and I've had months of dreaming about him and at least a month of worrying about what to do about the baby. But now he was here and part of me just wanted to lose myself in the pleasure he could give me.

Except reality is crashing in and I'm standing in his arms, trembling with the aftershocks of the orgasm he gave me, yet nothing has changed. He's still the stranger I met in Singapore. The stranger who demanded that I marry him.

I rip my mouth from his and try to push myself away from him, but he won't let me. His arm tightens around my waist, keeping me against him, and it's probably a good thing since I'm not quite steady enough on my feet to stand without help. The hard line of his arousal is pressing into the sensitive place between my thighs and I'm suddenly fiercely glad that he's as affected as I am by this heat between us.

'No,' he murmurs. 'Don't do that.'

I lean my forehead against his chest, not wanting to

meet his intense black gaze, not quite yet, and I feel a gentle hand settle on the back of my head, stroking my hair. There is something inexplicably soothing about it, but I don't want to be soothed. It's Christmas Eve and my brother will be home, and I won't be there to see him. I'm in Sicily, kidnapped by the father of my child and he's talking about things like marriage, and I don't know what to do.

Don't go to pieces, not here, not now.

No, I can't. I can't give into my rising panic. I have to hold it together, because it's not just about me any more. I have a child to consider now.

'We can talk about this tomorrow,' he says, still stroking my hair. 'You need to be tucked up in bed.' There's a roughness in his voice that betrays the effect what he did to me has had on him, and a part of me wants to use that, give him a taste of his own medicine. A way to make me feel strong and not as weak as I feel right now. And I hate feeling weak. I hate feeling the way I did when Ulysses first rescued me, an abused little girl afraid of her own shadow.

Fragile, that's what my brother called me, and that's how he treated me too, and while fragile is certainly what I was all those years ago, I'm not fragile now and I won't be treated like a child.

So I gather my strength and this time when I push away from him, I'm strong enough that I slip out of his imprisoning arm and take a few steps back.

He doesn't protest, but his black eyes burn as he looks at me.

'Don't patronise me,' I say to him flatly. 'And don't

think that one orgasm is going to change my mind. I'm still not marrying you.'

He stares at me for a long moment. 'We can talk about that tomorrow. You look dead on your feet.'

I fold my arms and stare back, trying to get my brain to work again, because I have to think. This conversation is important and some of the things he's said to me don't quite make sense. Such as 'rumours' of me being a prisoner and how he bribed my doctor. The speed at which he brought me here, which could naturally be that he didn't want to deal with Ulysses, and who could blame him? Ulysses isn't a man you cross lightly. Then again, Rafael Santangelo looks a match for him, so it can't be that he's afraid of what Ulysses might do. He's kidnapped me on Christmas Eve and now he's demanding marriage…

'No,' I say, gripping tight to my courage. 'We'll talk now. Tell me the real reason I'm here, Rafael. It's not just for the sake of the baby, is it?'

A muscle in the side of his jaw leaps and he mutters something vicious in Italian under his breath. 'Don't push me, dragonfly.'

'I'm not pushing you. I'm only asking you a question.'

'And I am choosing not to answer.'

'Why not? Are you afraid of my brother? Is that it?'

His mouth lifts in a sneer. 'No. Why the hell would I be afraid of him?'

A fine thread of contempt winds through his voice and it betrays him. My brother has enemies—that's why I have a security detail, after all—and perhaps

Rafael Santangelo is one of them. Why else would he sneer? If so, I need to find out and fast. Before he touches me again.

'If you know what's good for you, you would be,' I say. 'You know him, don't you?'

Rafael's dark eyes are unwavering. 'Don't ask questions, Olympia. Especially when you might not like the answers.'

'I'll be the judge of that.' I lift my chin. 'I know you're hiding something. I can't believe you'd go to all the trouble of kidnapping me just because of an accidental pregnancy. It's something to do with him, isn't it?'

Again that muscle leaps in his jaw, his eyes glittering like onyx in the light. He looks dangerous, as if he might do anything, anything at all, and by rights I should be terrified of him. But strangely, I'm not. I keep thinking of his hand stroking my hair gently and the sweetness of the kiss he gave me as I came apart in his arms. He's not going to hurt me or our baby.

'I have nothing to say to you.' His tone is edged and sharp. 'I told you we're not having this conversation and—'

'I didn't want to go that night in Singapore,' I interrupt, instinct telling me that if I want something from him, I'll have to give him something first. 'I wanted to stay with you.'

Something flickers in the darkness of his eyes and he glances away. He knows I'm giving him a piece of myself, I'm sure of it, and if he's any kind of businessman, he'll know what it means.

Abruptly, he lets out a breath and glances back. 'Very well, if you want the truth, I'll give it to you. Yes, this has something to do with your brother. Years ago Vulcan Energy was pushing into Italy, buying up companies and ripping them apart. My family owned a wind farm. It was my father's passion project and he'd poured a fortune into it, so it was easy meat for Zakynthos. Vulcan Energy swallowed it whole. My father tried to recover and start again, but the debts he ran up were too high, and eventually he was ruined.'

Rafael's voice is hard and cold and flat. 'He killed himself not long after that, leaving my mother and me saddled with his debt. My mother had a job at the local bakery, but her wages weren't nearly enough to cover the debt, so she began to court men who had money, hoping they might pay for her…"company".'

The bitterness in his voice becomes acute. 'I couldn't bear for her to do that, so I found work myself, at Atlas Construction as a labourer. It was run by the *consiglieri* of the boss of one of the more powerful of the *Cosa Nostra* families and eventually I did jobs for him.' He pauses, his gaze roving over my face. 'When I told you I was a bad man, I meant it. The things I've done…' He stops, and my heart kicks against my ribs. 'I hold your brother directly responsible for my family's ruin and for my own, and since he took my family from me, I'm going to take his from him.'

A long, cold, barbed thread of shock winds through me and pulls tight.

My brother is a ruthless man and I know this. I also know that he too worked for a local crime family, in

Athens, making contacts and earning the money he needed to rescue me. He didn't stop after I was rescued, though. He kept on making contacts and earning money, building Vulcan Energy, building his power so he could keep us both safe.

I never ask him about what he did in the bad old days in Athens and he never talks about it. But I know what those crime families get up to, and I can only imagine it's the same in Sicily.

I want to tell him that it couldn't have been Ulysses who ruined his family, but I can't. My brother wants what he wants and he'll go to any lengths to get it, and if that means swallowing some small family company then that's what he'll do.

I swallow, my mouth dry. 'So, what? You're taking me from him? I'm your revenge?'

He doesn't hesitate. 'Yes. I'd initially planned—'

'Wait,' I interrupt, that cold thread of shock pulling tighter. 'You were planning this? How long, Rafael?'

The lines of his face have hardened, the fierce heat that burned in his black eyes now stone cold. 'Since before Singapore.'

The needle of hurt that slid between my ribs that night in his hotel suite slides in again, even sharper, even deeper. 'You approached me intentionally at the gala?'

Again, there is no hesitation. 'My intent was to make a connection with you and then gradually get closer to you.'

I can't seem to catch my breath. 'And that night, in your hotel room...'

Only now does his gaze flicker. 'That was...unexpected. I didn't plan on that happening.'

I feel winded, as if he's punched me in the gut. 'But you decided to sleep with me anyway.'

'Yes.' He bites off the word.

So why did he send you away afterwards?

I fight through the remaining shreds of orgasm clouding my brain, because if that night had been as calculated as he said, then surely having me stay the night would further his cause more than making me leave? Or am I just clutching at straws? At anything to make me feel less used? Less of a victim?

'So why didn't you make me stay?' I ask.

He is silent and for a moment I don't think he's going to answer. Then he says, 'Because you were not what I expected, nor was my response to you. You were innocent, dragonfly, and I found I had more of a conscience than I thought.'

I shiver. That should make me feel better, yet it doesn't. He still used me. I'm still the innocent, sheltered victim, too stupid to know what he was doing.

'So why am I standing here in your house, then?' I ask, struggling to understand. 'Clearly you have *less* of a conscience than you thought.'

'I remembered that I hadn't used a condom and so I wanted to be sure you weren't pregnant. But...you were. And I am not a man who disregards an opportunity when it falls into his lap.'

I understand then, what he wants, what he's trying to do, and it feels as if a bucket of ice water has been emptied over my head. 'You want to marry me because

I'm Ulysses's heir,' I say and it's not a question. 'And then our child will be yours, with the potential to take over Vulcan Energy.'

He says nothing, but doesn't look away, and I can see the truth in his eyes. Yes, that's exactly what he intends, and it makes sense. Ulysses is an infamous bachelor. He's sworn never to marry and never to have children and everyone knows that.

Rafael told you that he is a bad man, remember?

I turn away from him then, the feeling of being punched in the gut getting stronger. Ulysses told me that there was a reason I had a security detail whenever I went out of the house. A reason why he was always so concerned with my safety. He had enemies and I was a chink in his armour that had to be protected at all costs.

I thought he was being too over-protective, that he was suffocating me, preventing me from living my life, and I'd pleaded with him to let me go to Singapore because I was tired of my life in the villa at home. I wanted to see different things, meet different people, and he'd agreed.

I was so happy, so thrilled, and when I'd escaped my security to go to Rafael's hotel suite, I'd felt so pleased with myself, thinking I was a woman of the world. But I was stupid. I'd let myself be taken advantage of, just the way Ulysses had feared, and now here I am, a prisoner. A tool to be used by Rafael to take my brother down.

'So that's all I am to you?' I ask into the suffocating quiet, staring at the white wall in front of me. 'An "opportunity"?' I don't know why this is so painful. Rafael shouldn't matter to me in any way, because, as he's already pointed out more than once, he's a stranger to me. And what we'd shared that night was only sex, nothing more, and yet...

You were a sop to your brother's guilt and now you're a tool for his demise.

My voice sounds weak, the questions pathetic, and suddenly I'm tired of all of this. Tired of being used by the men in my life, tired of being Ulysses's china doll, and tired of being a tool for Rafael's revenge.

He can't make me marry him and I won't let him. I won't let him use our child as a threat to hold over Ulysses's head either.

'Yes,' he says implacably. 'You're a means to an end, Olympia. But I can make things comfortable for you. I can make you—'

'*You* can't make me do anything,' I interrupt sharply, turning around to face him. 'And you're right. This conversation is at an end. Now show me where I'm to sleep tonight.'

CHAPTER NINE

Rafael

IT'S CHRISTMAS DAY and I'm standing in the kitchen putting the last touches on the omelette I've made for Olympia's breakfast. Full of cheese and ham and peppers, good protein for her and the baby. There's orange juice and fresh brioche too. I didn't sleep much last night, so I got up at dawn to cook. My mother was of the opinion that all grown men should know how to feed themselves, so she taught me how. I don't do it at lot since these days I'm often travelling, but when I have the time to cook, it always calms me.

Olympia will be hungry when she wakes since she refused dinner last night. After our argument, when she demanded to know where she'd be sleeping, I took her upstairs to my bedroom, whereupon she promptly closed the door on me then locked it.

I'd stood there a couple of moments, debating whether kicking down the door in a fury was reasonable or whether it was better to walk away, because, after all, what did I expect? After I'd told her she was merely a means to an end? She was angry and she had a right to be.

In the end, good sense prevailed and I walked away. Later, after putting the meal my housekeeper had left for me into the oven to warm up, I went back upstairs and knocked on the door to tell her that she needed to eat. But she didn't respond other than to tell me in no uncertain terms to go away.

Sleeping alone in one of the guest rooms was not how I'd envisaged my first Christmas Eve with her, but I certainly wasn't going to force myself on her. That wouldn't advance my cause, especially when she'd made it very clear she wasn't going to marry me.

I shouldn't have told her the truth about my revenge plans last night, but she'd pushed me and I'd lost patience. She'd already made it clear that marrying me willingly wasn't on the cards, so I wasn't going to lose anything by telling her. Of course, now she knows my real motivations, she *definitely* won't marry me—she'll want to protect her brother—but I'm sure I can convince her otherwise. I just need to think about how.

Telling her she was just a means to an end didn't help.

No and that was another thing I shouldn't have said. But I'd had to say it. I'd had to be clear about my intentions and about what she was to me, because while there's attraction between us, there can't be anything more and I won't pretend that there could be. I have never wanted a relationship, not when I have to give all my attention to my company and my revenge plans. Besides, love makes everything far more complicated than it needs to be and my life is much simpler without it.

I go over other options in my head as I arrange her breakfast on a tray. I could give her money to marry me and promise her a life of luxury but, with her brother being as rich as Midas, I have a feeling that won't move her.

The other, more logical option is use to the physical attraction between us. It's still burning as bright and hot as it did that night in Singapore, and she wasn't proof against it last night. She came apart so beautifully in my arms, clinging to the lapels of my coat as if clinging to life itself.

Using sex would certainly be a much more pleasurable way to convince her than anything else, and one I'd very much enjoy myself.

I pick the tray full of breakfast up and leave the kitchen, making my way upstairs to the upper hallway. The door to my bedroom is still firmly closed. Since I'm holding the tray, I kick the door with my foot. 'Wake up, dragonfly,' I call. 'I have your breakfast here and you need to eat.'

There is a silence and I wonder if she's still asleep. Then I wonder if she's all right, that perhaps something has happened to her in the night, something to do with the baby. I kick the door again, harder this time. 'Olympia,' I say, trying to keep the concern from my voice. 'Talk to me. Let me know you're okay at least.'

Again, there's silence and I'm just about to put down the tray and kick the door in when there's a fumbling on the other side and the sound of a lock being turned.

Then the door opens a crack and she's standing there, glaring angrily at me.

I can't deny the relief that fills me at the sight. Her long black hair is tousled from sleep and she's still wearing her stretchy black dress. It's looking a little creased and I wonder if she's slept in it, not that it detracts from her inherent sex appeal. Just looking at her I can feel my body respond with predictable speed.

'What do you want?' she demands. 'I haven't changed my mind if that's what you think.'

'I don't think that,' I say mildly, since arguing with her will likely result in the door of my own bedroom slamming shut in my face again. 'I'm only here to bring you breakfast and, since you missed dinner last night, you're going to need it. Or at least, the baby will.'

Her gaze drops to the tray and, on cue, her stomach growls.

'Come, dragonfly,' I say. 'Let me bring this in.'

Still glaring, she lets out a long breath then finally steps away from the door, allowing me inside. My big four-poster bed is against one wall, opposite the windows, and I glance at it to see if the sheets are disturbed. They are, which is good. It means she slept in it and since my bed is extremely comfortable, she'll have had a good sleep.

I move over to it and set the tray down on the bed. She has gone to stand by one of the windows that looks out over the cliff to the sea. Her back is rigid, her arms folded, every inch of her furious negation.

'You can call your brother this morning,' I tell her,

searching for something that will mollify her enough to come over to the bed and eat.

'Merry Christmas to you too,' she says tartly.

I don't need the reminder. I know exactly what day it is. I even have the tree downstairs, hung with the decorations my mother would take out of storage every year. I'd help her put them on the tree and then, afterwards, I'd sit beneath it reading, while she made me hot chocolate.

My mother has gone now and my father along with her, but I still decorate the tree every year with our family's decorations, even if I no longer sit beneath it drinking hot chocolate.

'Merry Christmas,' I offer stiffly. 'Come and eat.'

She turns slowly from the window and studies me, then glances at the tray again. 'You can go now. I'd rather you didn't stay to watch me eat.'

'Too bad. I need to see you actually eat the food.'

Temper flashes in her eyes. 'I'm not a child, Rafael.'

'Then stop acting like one.'

Her mouth hardens, and no matter that her hair is all over the place, her dress is creased, and she's scowling at me as if I'm the devil himself, she's still the loveliest thing I've ever seen in my entire life.

'I'm not going to give in, you know,' she says as she crosses over to the bed. 'No matter how many omelettes you make me.' She peers at the tray, then sits down on the edge of the bed and picks up the brioche. It's fresh and still warm and I can see the flicker of pleasure cross her face as she daintily pulls it apart and puts a bit in her mouth.

So, she's already guessed that I have ulterior motives in making her breakfast, and she's not wrong about them. I *do* have ulterior motives. But she's wrong in that it isn't food I've decided to use in order to get what I want from her.

Though maybe, given how much of a turn-on it is to watch her pull apart the brioche and put it between her red lips, I could combine the two. Sex and food would certainly be interesting. But I have to be careful how I do it. Patience is not my strong suit, but I can be patient when the situation calls for it.

I need to make her desperate for me, desperate enough to agree to anything I ask and not think of the consequences.

'Agree to marry me and I'll let you speak to your brother,' I say, testing the ground a little as I come over to where she's sitting.

She glances up at me, popping another piece of brioche into her mouth and chewing thoughtfully. 'Oh, you'll *let* me, will you? Hmmm.' She pulls off another piece and eats it, still looking at me. 'Okay. Fine. I'll do it.'

A ripple of shock goes through me. Given how she held her ground last night, I wasn't expecting her to give in so quickly or so easily. I eye her with some scepticism. 'You'll marry me, you mean?'

'Yes.'

'Just like that?'

'Yes.' She wipes her hands very ostentatiously down her dress then gestures imperiously at me. 'Come on. Give me the phone.'

I'm doubtful that she meant what she said, but still, I promised her, so I pull my phone from my pocket, unlock it and hand it to her.

'Not much of a kidnapper, are you?' she says as she takes the phone from me and begins typing in her brother's number. 'I don't have anything to wear. The least you could have done is get me a change of clothes.'

'Give me some credit,' I say coolly. 'I've ordered you a whole wardrobe. It'll arrive the day after tomorrow.'

I'm satisfied when I see surprise flicker across her face as she raises the phone to her ear, then she blinks. 'Don't get angry, Ulysses,' she says, sounding calm. 'There's a few things I need to say to you.'

If I was a decent man, I'd give her some privacy, but I'm not a decent man. I want to be in the room when she tells him where she is and why.

It's pleasing to me that he's angry, because that's what I'd hoped. I want him angry. I want him afraid. I want him desperate to have his sister back, and then to deny him.

'Listen to me,' she continues. 'I have something to tell you.'

I fold my arms, continuing to stare down at her, watching her face for what, I don't know.

'I...can't spend Christmas with you,' she says and, though she sounds calm, there's a slight catch in her voice.

It hits me then that, while I know what she means to her brother, I don't know what he means to her. Obviously she loves him, but she sounds a little...upset.

It's Christmas Day, you bastard. Don't you think

she might have feelings about being separated from her only family?

'No,' she says. 'I'm not in any danger. So you can stand down the battle stations.'

A whisper of unfamiliar shame ghosts through me. I have never cared about other people's feelings. Since my parents' deaths I've let no one matter enough for me to care, but now I feel some discomfort at the thought of her being alone on Christmas Day, with only me for company.

'Look, I really am safe, Ulysses. I'm not in danger at all. I just…can't come to you right now.' Her amber gaze flickers in my direction. 'I've got a few things to sort out.'

I study her again, my discomfort growing. She's wearing the only dress she has, her hair a mess, the little round bump of her stomach making her seem even smaller and more delicate, and I've torn her away from her family. I, of all people, know the pain of that so intimately and yet I've done to her what her brother did to me and that's…not a good feeling.

'I know, I know.' She sighs then mutters something filthy. 'I didn't want to have to tell you like this.' Her hand comes to rest gently on her stomach 'No. I'm not going to tell you where I am or who I'm with, because then you'll start looking for me, and I don't need that drama, okay?'

That distracts me from my discomfort. So she's not going to tell him where she is? Interesting. I wonder why she doesn't want him looking for her, because she sure as hell doesn't want to be here with me.

There is a pause and I can hear his voice, deep and furious down the other end of the line. 'Ulysses,' she says cutting into his tirade. 'I'm pregnant.'

She told me he didn't know and I'm pleased that he didn't. That I knew before he did.

'You're going to be an uncle,' she continues, a husk in her voice, her fingers spreading protectively over her bump. 'It's early days, but I wanted you to know, and I didn't want you to worry about me. I'm with the father and I'm safe, but please, please, don't come looking for me.'

'Enough,' I snap, tired of the conversation and the faint threads of emotion in her voice that are making me feel things I don't want to feel. 'Give the phone to me.'

She glares at me angrily. 'I haven't finished.'

'I don't care.' I snatch the phone from her hand. 'She's with me, Zakynthos,' I growl down the phone. 'Rafael Santangelo. And I'm the father of her child. Merry Christmas, motherfucker.' Then I hit the end button.

'Why did you give him your name?' she demands. 'He'll find you, you know. You won't be able to escape him.'

'What do you care?' I fire back. 'Don't you want him to rescue you?'

Her gaze flickers, the fire of her temper blazing high. 'Rescue me?' she echoes, as if she's never heard of anything so ridiculous. 'I'm not Rapunzel, Rafael. I don't need any rescuing.'

Looking at her, all hot temper and cold steel, I can well believe it. She might seem a fragile, delicate flower, but this rose has sharp thorns and she's not afraid to use them.

'Fine,' I say. 'You're not Rapunzel, but I'm not a man easily frightened. I can handle your brother. I told him who I was because I wanted him to know that I'm the father of his niece or nephew.'

'Why?' Her gaze is searching. 'He sometimes talks about his business, but I'm pretty sure he's never mentioned your name.'

He wouldn't. He doesn't know I exist. The demise of my family's company meant nothing to him. Just another small company crushed beneath the weight of a multinational conglomerate, and who cares about the human cost? Who cares about the consequences to the people whose lives are ripped apart by it?

'And that's why.' I can't keep the relish out of my tone. 'I want him to know who took you and who'll eventually own his fucking company.'

'Excuse me,' she says coolly, drawing herself up. '*I* will eventually own his fucking company.'

'No, you won't. Not after you marry me.'

'But I'm not going to marry you,' she disagrees, oh, so calmly.

I stare at her. 'You said you would. You agreed to—'

'I lied.' Her amber eyes are challenging and it strikes me suddenly that by rights she should be afraid. I've taken her away from her brother, from the only home she's ever known, and now she's hundreds of miles away from him and from safety. Yet there's no fear in her eyes, only challenge, and something hot and raw rises inside me.

I take one step to the edge of the bed where she's sitting, and even though I'm towering over her, she only stares back at me, that challenge still glinting in her eyes, and I'm helpless to resist it. I know one way to get her begging, to get her agreeing to anything I ask, anything I demand.

I bend and take the tray off the bed, placing it on the bedside table.

'Hey,' she says. 'I haven't finished.'

'Too bad.' I step closer and lean down over her, forcing her backwards and down across the mattress. She is breathing fast as I place my hands on either side of her head, her gaze dipping to my mouth and up again, the colour rising in her cheeks. 'I haven't finished either,' I murmur, then I cover her lips with my own.

CHAPTER TEN

Olympia

I LIE BACK on the mattress, trembling as his mouth comes down on mine. My heart is beating hard and fast, and the touch of his lips makes the breath catch in my throat. He's gentle, his kiss coaxing and hot, but it's not me who's surrendering and I can't escape the intense satisfaction that coils tight inside me.

I used his own tactics against him, lying about marrying him, and he was the one who broke in the end, not me. No doubt he thinks he can make me do what he wants using sex, but if so, he's in for a surprise.

My anger flickers as I open my mouth to let him in. He tastes of dark coffee and chocolate, and it's delicious. I want to grab him, devour him, show him that the one thing I'm not is a tool for his use.

Ironically, it was talking to Ulysses that solidified my determination. I've heard him be funny, frustrated, impatient, and furious, but I've never heard him be afraid. I didn't want to be the reason for that fear, but that choice was taken out of my hands by Rafael. I didn't want to tell Ulysses about the pregnancy like that either, but again, that was Rafael's fault.

Then again, if Rafael hadn't taken me, would I have ever confessed to Ulysses? I'd still be there in the villa beside the ocean, still, in many ways, a prisoner of my own fear and indecision.

I'm not there now though. Rafael took me away, made me search within myself to find the strength I didn't know I had, and sure enough, it was there. Strength to save me and my baby, to stand up to him and maybe bend him to my will even as he's trying to bend me to his.

I managed it last night, locking him out of his own bedroom, which was incredibly satisfying. I didn't want to fall asleep in his far too comfortable bed so quickly, but I must have been more tired than I thought, because I did.

My dreams, though, were hot and fevered, and I woke up aching. My body is Sleeping Beauty woken by a kiss and now hungry for nothing but more of them, everywhere, all over. Especially when I'd pulled open the door to find him standing on the other side, holding a tray full of delicious-looking breakfast.

Yet it was he who made me even more hungry, dressed in worn jeans and a black T-shirt, his short black hair standing up as if he'd run a hand through it one too many times. His dark eyes met mine and I'd felt the need rise in me, watched it flare in his gaze, too.

I always planned for him to do this, to take me down onto the bed and kiss me senseless, but I'd also planned to be the one in control of it, to be in control of myself and to stay in control.

Yet as his hot mouth devastates me with a kiss so sensual I can't resist placing my hands against his hard chest, I can feel that control slipping. His body is as hot as his mouth and I want to lick him all over, explore him the way I never got to do in Singapore.

'Marry me, dragonfly,' he whispers against my lips. 'I'll make you feel so good every night. You'll never go to bed hungry.'

I want to tell him no, I'm not going to marry him and he's a fool if he thinks I will, but that kiss of his…hot chocolate, whisky, sex and sin, everything I'm craving and I can't help but whisper in return, 'Make me.' And something in me wants him to. Something in me wants him to convince me that marrying him would be a good thing. I'm not immune to his promises. The thought of having him every night is…seductive. Too seductive.

His mouth trails kisses along my jaw and down my neck, and he gives a low laugh. 'Is that a challenge?'

'Yes,' I breathe, the words escaping before I can stop them. 'Convince me.'

He lifts his head, the look in his eyes scorching me to the bone. 'Are you sure that's what you want? I can be *very* convincing.'

I know exactly how convincing he can be and exactly how weak I am in the face of it. But to hell with that. If there's another way, a better way, to test my own strength against his I don't know it. I can't compete with him anywhere else but this room, this bed, and there's a piece of me that wants to test him and test myself too.

'Don't make the mistake of thinking I'm a doormat, Rafael,' I tell him huskily. 'Or a sheltered virgin who knows nothing about the real world. I've been through things you can't imagine.'

His gaze sharpens. 'What things?'

Silly of me to mention that, because I don't want to talk about it, not now and not here. So I reach up, sliding my fingers into the raw silk of his hair and holding on, pulling his mouth back where it belongs. On mine.

He is rigid in my grip for only a minute and then his mouth opens and he's devouring me as hungrily as I'm devouring him. But he won't have forgotten. What I've said has sparked his interest and I know what happens when his interest is sparked. He'll get it out of me at some stage.

But that's not now and so I lose myself in the heated glory of his kiss. His weight on me is heavy, yet not uncomfortable. It's a barrier between me and the world, a brick wall protecting me. Hard and strong and impenetrable.

I spread my legs so he can settle between them, the hard ridge of his cock pressing down right where it feels so good, making me want to writhe against him, intensify my pleasure.

'Ah, dragonfly,' he whispers against my neck. 'If I give you what you want right now, that'll leave me with nothing to bargain with.'

'So?' I whisper back. 'It'll cost you nothing.'

'I know exactly what it'll cost me.' He presses a hot

kiss on my throat then lifts his head and reaches for the drawer in the bedside table, pulling it open and extracting a handful of silky fabric. 'And sadly for you, I'm a much better businessman than that.' He stares down at me, his dark eyes blazing, and I don't miss the challenge in them. 'You want me to convince you then here's my first argument.' He holds up the fabric. 'Submit yourself to me, dragonfly. Submit and I'll give you everything you ever wanted.'

My heart is hammering as I glance at the handful of silk. They're scarves, soft-looking and brightly coloured, and I suspect I know what he wants to do with them.

Well, I wanted to test myself against him, didn't I? A whisper of trepidation chases across my skin, but not because of what he wants to do to me. It's more because I can feel the intense throb between my thighs and I fear that I want this very much. Too much. What could he make me agree to if I do this for him? What would I give up for the pleasure he can give me?

Do you care?

I don't like the thought of being bound, it makes me think of myself all those years ago and how my foster mother would tie me up and put me in a closet every night because she didn't want me wandering. I still remember the suffocating blackness of that closet and how the plastic of the zip ties would dig into my wrists, making it hard for me to sleep, and how sometimes I'd panic, feeling as if I was being buried alive.

But this isn't the same. There is no blackness, only the cold morning sun coming through the windows, and the ties are silk, not plastic, and the man who wants to bind me is looking at me as if there is nothing more important than me giving him this. And it *is* a gift. He's not taking it from me the way my abusive foster parents did or forcing me to do it. He's asking me and challenging me at the same time, and how can I help but give this to him?

Those memories of being bound are terrible, of me feeling weak and helpless and small. Of knowing that I didn't matter to the people who were supposed to care for me. That I was alone in the world except for the brother who'd been taken away from me.

But right here, right now, Rafael can give me new memories. Better memories. Memories of pleasure, because I have no doubt this will give me pleasure. Memories of him looking at me as if I was the most beautiful, the most precious thing in the universe to him.

This won't trap you. This will set you free.

I meet his hot gaze and I don't flinch away. And I raise my hands, my wrists pressed together. The look in his eyes flares and I can see the triumph and satisfaction flicker across his beautiful features, as well as a fleeting relief. He was hoping for this and it makes me feel good that I've pleased him.

'First,' he murmurs and shifts, taking the hem of my dress and sliding it up. I help him, my heartbeat accelerating as he uncovers me, pulling the dress off and over my head. He gets rid of my underwear and then I'm lying on the bed naked as he takes my hands and winds the silk around my wrists.

I'm breathing fast and he's watching me, gauging my reactions, and I know suddenly and completely that if I was afraid he would stop. I wouldn't even have to say the words. He'd know just by looking at me.

Slowly he lifts my bound wrists above my head and back, and, with a deft movement, ties them to the headboard of the bed. Then he stares down at me and the hunger in his dark eyes robs me of breath. I'm naked and bound, and at his mercy, and yet I don't feel powerless. I don't feel weak. He's staring at me as if I'm a feast set out for his pleasure and he doesn't know where to start because everything looks good to him.

It's incredibly erotic.

He lifts a hand and runs it gently down my body, stroking my skin, mapping my curves. Light touches, teasing touches. Then he stretches himself over me, on his hands and knees, looking down into my eyes as he lifts a hand and cups one breast. My breathing gets faster and he continues to watch me as he teases my hardening nipple with his thumb, circling it then pinching gently. 'Such a beautiful dragonfly,' he murmurs as he touches me. 'Do you like this? Do you like being mine?'

I want to tell him that I'm not his, but as his mouth settles in the hollow of my throat and he slides a hand over my stomach, I lose the words I wanted to say. Because yes, I do like this. I like him calling me beautiful. I like being his.

His hand slips between my thighs and I gasp as he touches me, his fingers exploring the wet folds of my sex, his mouth an ember on my throat, my neck, my collarbones and then down. He uses his mouth to feast on me, his tongue teasing the hard points of my breasts as he slides a finger into me and then another.

I gasp aloud as the pleasure spiders out like a crack in a mirror, carving lines and fissures in me, making me pant. I'm aware of the soft silk around my wrists and the feeling of constraint only adds to the sensation, even as I pull against it slightly, wanting to touch him the way he's touching me.

I lift my hips to his hand, wanting more than his fingers, needing more. 'Please,' I whisper. 'Rafael, please.'

But he shakes his head, his gaze scorching. 'Promise me you'll marry me, dragonfly,' he murmurs. 'Promise me and I'll give you what you want.'

'I could lie,' I pant, unable to stop moving as he continues his maddening stroke between my thighs. 'I could lie again.'

'You could,' he agrees. 'But if you lie, I'll never touch you again.' His hand slows and then withdraws. 'You'll feel like this, desperate and aching and unfulfilled.' His stare is intense and there are flames behind his eyes. 'It'll be painful to be without me, dragonfly. No other man can give you this. No other man can make you feel this way.'

I'm panting, unable to keep still, and a part of me knows that he's right. That no other man can make me feel this way, and in fact I wouldn't let any other man bind me this way. Touch me this way. And even the thought of doing this with anyone else leaves me cold.

Still, I can't give in straight away or fold like a house

of cards. Sex is only part of a marriage and we need more than that, especially when a child is involved.

He trails his mouth down to the slight curve of my stomach where our child rests and he touches me reverently, as if I'm holy, precious. 'Would you lie to me about this, hmmm?' He lifts his head and raises himself again, so he's over me but no part of his body is touching mine. 'Can you bear it, dragonfly? Can you bear to feel this way for ever?' There is demand in his eyes and it compels the truth from me.

'No,' I whisper. 'I can't.'

He runs his fingertips down the length of my body, his gaze pinning me to the mattress, his light teasing touch making me tremble. 'Then promise me,' he orders. 'Promise me that you'll marry me and I'll give you this whenever you want. I'll give you as much pleasure as you can handle and more.'

I'm panting now as his fingers slip once again between my thighs and he begins to stroke and caress me again. My thoughts are slippery and I don't want to think, I want to give myself up completely to the pleasure he's giving me, but I can't. Not yet. I need him to give me something too.

'Leave my brother alone,' I say, my voice husky. 'Leave my brother alone and I'll marry you.'

He goes still, the look in his eyes getting sharper. I'm naked and bound and beneath him, and I should feel weak, helpless and in his power, yet I don't.

I can see the hunger in his eyes and I know how badly he wants this, how badly he wants me. He's in my power now and as he used pleasure to get me to do what he wants, I'm using it to get what I want now.

Do you really understand what you're asking him to give up?

Only then does a fragile thread of doubt wind through me. His father died and his mother sold herself to repay the family debt, and I saw in his eyes how that affected him. He's damaged, just as I have been damaged, and who am I to tell him what he should give up?

Except he wants it from the person I love most in the world, wants to destroy him, and I can't let that happen, no matter how badly Rafael has been hurt. My brother, too, has been hurt, has been damaged. His need to grow Vulcan has more to do with protecting me than actual greed, and by taking me from him, Rafael has started a war he has no concept of.

Revenge won't help him, just as my brother's guilt hasn't helped him, and if I allow it to go on, this might affect the child I'm carrying, and the next generation will carry the same damage.

I can't let that happen. It has to stop somewhere. It has to stop with me.

'I'll give you whatever you want,' he says, his voice hard. 'Except that.'

'That's sad,' I say steadily. 'Because that's what I want.'

A muscle flicks in his jaw as he stares down at me and, obeying some instinct, I shift beneath him, a slow undulation of my body. His attention flickers at the movement, and I see the flames in his eyes burn higher.

He's hungry for me, I know that. But is he hungry enough to give me this?

'I could just take what I want now,' he growls, his hot temper showing in his voice. 'While you're tied up and unable to stop me.'

It's an empty threat and we both know that. He won't touch me if I don't want him to. 'You could,' I agree. 'But you won't.' And I make another undulating movement, lifting my chest so the tips of my breasts brush the cotton of his T-shirt, and then my hips, pressing the needy heat between my thighs to the hard ridge behind the zip of his jeans.

'Fuck,' he mutters, the look in his eyes glazing. 'Olympia…you don't know what you're asking for.'

He's wrong. I know. 'I don't care,' I murmur. 'Those are my terms. Now make a decision and put us both out of our misery.'

He stays there, statue-still, fury and frustration blazing in his dark eyes, and for a moment I wonder if I've been too hasty with my demands. If he wants his revenge on Ulysses more than he wants me, but then he mutters another curse and gets off the bed.

But he's not leaving. He claws his clothes off with impatient hands and then he's back on the bed again, the sun shining through the windows showing me every glorious inch of his naked body. Hard, carved muscle, velvety olive skin, a scattering of crisp black hair across his chest. He's the epitome of male beauty. Michelangelo would have loved to sculpt him. He would have put David to shame.

My breath escapes as he kneels between my thighs,

his hands sliding beneath my rear, the heat of his palms against my hot skin making me gasp.

'Your promise,' he growls as he lifts my hips. 'All the words, dragonfly.'

'Yes,' I say shakily, already trembling with anticipation. 'Yes, I'll marry you, Rafael. I promise.' I hold his gaze. 'Your turn.'

The muscle in the side of his jaw flicks again, anger clear in his eyes along with the heat of desire. There's a silence and I know he's struggling with the words. But I want them and I won't give him what he wants until I hear them, and he knows that.

'I'll leave your brother alone,' he grits out. 'I promise, Olympia.'

He doesn't wait after that. He grips my hips and I feel him press into me, sliding deep inside, and the intensity of the sensation almost strangles me. I cry out hoarsely, the press and stretch of him incredible.

He growls and begins to move, deep and slow, making me writhe, pulling against the headboard, wanting to touch him. He leans forward, looking down at me, and I'm lost in the darkness of his eyes. He's hypnotic, mesmerising, the thrust of hips sending pleasure spiralling through me, layer upon layer of it.

He's merciless, he sends me over the edge and then builds me up again, making me scream and pant, until I'm nothing but a creature made out of desire and there is nothing in the world but him.

And when I explode for the second time, he follows me.

CHAPTER ELEVEN

Rafael

I'M LYING IN BED, Olympia's warm and very naked body sprawled over mine, her hair a silky black storm over my chest as I sift long strands of it through my fingers.

I want to be furious about the promise she made me give her, to leave that bastard brother of hers alone, but she surprised me. I wasn't expecting her to shoot back a demand of her own, though I should have. She told me she wasn't a doormat, and even though I didn't need the reminder, I clearly underestimated her.

It was only that lying beneath me, naked and hungry, she should have been at my mercy. I didn't think I'd end up being at hers and yet she got that promise out of me somehow. I could have taken what I wanted—she wouldn't have been able to stop me, not with her hands tied—and I'd told her so. Yet she'd only looked at me and said with absolutely no doubt in her voice that I wouldn't, as if she knew me better than I knew myself.

And maybe she does. I've long since lost the privilege of having scruples or lines in the sand, and so one woman's request to stop chasing the revenge that has driven the last ten years of my life shouldn't have given me pause. Yet it did. And looking into her dark eyes I knew she was right. I wouldn't take what she wasn't willing to give, not without the promise she wanted, a promise she'd already given me. But still, I wanted her and in that moment I wanted her more than I wanted to take Ulysses Zakynthos down.

So I'd given her my promise, telling myself that I didn't mean it. That it was a lie, because after all I'd lied before and without any regrets whatsoever.

You meant it then and you mean it now.

Her hair slides like black silk through my fingers and I shove that thought away. What I will do is make sure of her promise to me before I take any action against Ulysses. I'll marry her, secure my heir and look at my options then.

'So,' I say into the heavy silence. 'Are you going to tell me what you meant?'

She shifts on me, hot silky skin sliding against mine, and my cock stirs, ready for another round. But I won't be distracted again so I ignore it. She said she'd been through 'things you can't imagine' and, since my imagination is excellent, I want to know exactly what she meant by that. It can't be anything bad, not when she's been sheltered all her life in her brother's villa on the Greek Riviera.

'About what?' She's sprawled over my chest, her fingers drawing little circles on my skin, her body warm and soft against mine.

'You said you'd "been through things".'

'Oh, that.' Her attention is on my chest, her fingertips tracing the scars from a knife fight I got into years ago. 'Seems like you've been through some things too.'

'A knife,' I say dismissively. 'I'm going to be your husband, dragonfly. Which means I need to know everything there is to know about my prospective wife.'

She glances up at me. 'Do you though? Do you really?'

'Olympia,' I say with a hint of impatience. 'You made me a promise.'

'To be your wife. Nothing else.'

Her eyes are full of challenge and I can sense the barrier behind them. A blank brick wall to keep people out.

Yes, they were bad things.

Something in my chest constricts. Her reluctance to tell me says it all, and suddenly I very much want to know what happened to her and make sure that if someone hurt her, I would hunt them to the ends of the earth to make them pay.

'Did your brother—?'

'No,' she says sharply, cutting me off. 'I told you, Ulysses would never hurt me.'

'Then who? Someone hurt you, didn't they?' Letting her hair go, I reach out and touch her cheek gently. 'Tell me, dragonfly.'

Much to my surprise and probably to hers too, her eyes fill with tears. She pushes herself away from me, making as if to leave, but I'm not letting her walk away again, especially not with those tears, so I reach for her, pulling her back into my arms and leaning against the headboard with her.

I don't want to press, because clearly this is painful, but also I want to know. I want her to trust me enough to tell me, even though I don't precisely know why I want that.

She's stiff in my arms, resisting, but I don't let go. 'If you don't want to tell me, that's okay,' I say in a gentler tone. 'I won't make you tell me. But I don't like to see you cry.'

She's silent, her head tucked under my chin, her cheek pressed to my chest. The stiffness in her body slowly ebbs until it's gone and I feel the dampness of a tear on my skin.

The constriction in my chest tightens still further.

'It's all right,' I murmur, pressing a kiss to the top of her silky head. 'You can keep your secrets, dragonfly. I won't force you.'

She takes a shaky breath and then says, her voice slightly muffled, 'It's been a long time since it happened. Years.'

I don't say anything, leaving her space to talk if she wants to, but I keep my arms tight around her, letting her know she's safe.

'My mother died when Ulysses and I were very young. We had no relatives so we had to go into foster care. Ulysses tried to make sure we stayed together, but we were split up in the end. My foster parents were… not kind.' Her voice is slightly hesitant, but there is a certain strength to it. 'They took me in because they wanted the money the state paid them to look after me, not actually me. My foster father used to drink a lot and he was a monster when he was drunk. He would beat me for no reason, just for the pleasure of it, I think. My foster mother would tie me up at night and lock me in a closet because she didn't want me "wandering around" at night.'

Nothing gets to me these days. I've seen and heard things that would scar the hardest of men, but the words Olympia says, in a clear, calm voice, chill me to the bone. Then, a second later, rage wells up inside me. My muscles tense and clearly she can feel it, because she suddenly shifts in my arms, pulling her head away so she can look up at me. Her cheeks are wet with her tears, but there's no fear in them, only a calm strength that takes my breath away. 'No,' she says. 'Don't be angry.'

'I'm not angry at you,' I force out, my fingers already curling into fists, wanting to hit something.

'I know you're not.' She's very calm. 'But I don't want to have to reassure you about something that happened to me.'

That stops me in my tracks and I have to recalibrate. Because no, she shouldn't have to deal with my anger on her behalf. Not given what she went through.

'I don't need you to reassure me,' I say, forcing back my anger. 'I'm just so sorry that happened to you, Olympia.'

She eyes me a long moment, then relaxes a little. 'It's okay,' she says. 'It's just... I had to deal with Ulysses's anger about it for years and, after a while, it's just another burden I have to bear.'

I can only imagine. Her brother might be a bastard

but it's always been clear that he cares very much for his sister.

I tighten the lid on my fury and lock it. 'How long were you there?'

'In that foster home? A couple of years, I think. Ulysses actually rescued me in the end. He and some… associates of his stole me away. He was old enough by then to look after me and I've stayed with him ever since.'

I hate Ulysses Zakynthos, but right in this moment I don't hate him. No, I'm thankful to him that he managed to rescue her and take her away from the people who were hurting her.

'I had nightmares for years afterwards,' she goes on. 'And I was…quite fragile for a long time too. But…' Her amber eyes darken as they meet mine, but her gaze is very steady. 'I know what people are capable of and I know what cruelty looks like. I wasn't ever sexually assaulted, because my foster father preferred girls over the age of twelve and so I wasn't quite old enough for him. But if I'd stayed there much longer, I would have been. You think I'm a sheltered, spoiled girl, but I'm not. I'm not innocent, Rafael.'

I am trying very hard to keep the lid on my fury and failing. And this time the fury is at myself for thinking that she was spoiled and sheltered. Because now I'm looking into her eyes and I can see the strength there, the brick wall, the iron at the centre of her. Whatever she went through as a child has hammered her on an anvil and made her into a sword, sharp and dangerous.

'I can see that,' I say. 'But just so we're clear, I never

thought you were a doormat, Olympia Zakynthos. And you made that very obvious from the second we met.'

Her gaze flickers as if I've said something unexpected and colour flushes her cheeks. 'I *am* sheltered,' she says. 'That much is true, but that's because Ulysses was kind of a helicopter parent as I was growing up.'

'Why?' I ask straight out. 'Did you need him to be?'

She sighs. 'I did… At first. I don't think any kid can go through something like that and not be traumatised in some way, and I was traumatised. But Ulysses got me some great doctors and I came through it.' Her gaze holds mine. 'Don't get me wrong, I'm grateful to him. I love him for rescuing me and for looking after me. For making sure the rest of my childhood was a good one. But I'm stronger now and I'm tired of being cosseted. I'm tired of being protected like a hothouse flower, and, more than anything else, I'm tired of being a living reminder of his failure to protect me and a receptacle for his guilt.'

Of course she's strong. I never thought of her as anything less and the evidence of that strength is sitting before me now, naked as the day she was born. I have a feeling that what she just told me was the tip of the iceberg of what those pathetic excuses for foster parents had done to her, and, if so, no wonder her brother is consumed with guilt. I would feel the same.

But now I truly understand why she doesn't want rage. If she's had to bear her brother's guilt and his anger for years, then she really doesn't need mine, no matter how hot and strong it burns.

'Then don't be,' I tell her. 'You're not his responsibility any more. When you're my wife, you'll be mine.'

She scowls. 'I'm not anyone's responsibility. I'm not a child.'

'I didn't say you were.' I scowl back. 'You'll be my responsibility, which means that whatever you want, whatever you need, just tell me and I'll give it to you.'

She eyes me. 'Ulysses used to say the same things to me, you know.'

Abruptly I understand why she's been so suspicious of me, not to mention so resistant. Her brother was protecting her, I can see that from what she said, but he's also been holding her back. He's been keeping her just like the hothouse flower she complained of being and now she's afraid I'll do the same thing.

I can't deny that a part of me agrees with her brother, wanting to keep her safe and protected and away from all harm. But I can also see the strength in the woman sitting on the bed. She had a horrendous thing happen to her, but she went through the fire and came out the other side, battle-hardened and even stronger. You can't keep a woman like that trapped in a castle like Rapunzel. She's not a princess, she's a knight, and knights are sent into battle, not kept within castle walls.

'But I'm not Ulysses,' I say flatly, meeting her stare. 'And I won't treat you like a cosseted child or a hothouse flower. I'll treat you like you're my wife, which you will be as soon as I can manage it.'

The darkness in her eyes flickers, the shadows in them moving, and I realise that I want to banish those shadows. I want to banish that look of suspicion, of guarded wariness. I want her to smile at me the way she did back in Singapore when our eyes first met. She's doing something to me and exactly what I don't know, but there's a part of me that doesn't care.

'And how would you treat a wife?' she asks, still confronting, still challenging. She's not going to let me get away with anything, is she?

And you like it.

Yes. I do. It's been a long time since I've been challenged by anyone, let alone one pretty, young woman, and the feral part of me is excited by the thought.

'I'll have to think about that,' I say. 'Since I haven't had a wife before.'

'You've never had a child before, either,' she says. 'Or perhaps you do and you're just not being honest—'

'No,' I say, cutting her off. 'I don't have any children. Like I told you, children have never been part of my plans.'

'I suppose having revenge and having kids are mutually exclusive,' she says and it's not a throwaway line. She means it.

She'll hold you to that promise you made her.

For the first time since I can remember, a cold, sharp doubt slides through me. I wanted it all, revenge, her and my child, but…using the baby in this way… That was the catalyst for all of this, my way to finally claim the justice I need for my father and my mother. To take what is important to Ulysses away from him the way he took my family from me, and yet…

It feels wrong to use her and the child as a weapon against her brother. To use their lives to hurt him. It feels petty and punitive and…selfish, almost. A betrayal of trust.

That shouldn't bother me, though. Who cares if I'm selfish or untrustworthy? After my father died, no one else's opinion mattered. I don't know why I'm letting it matter now, but I am.

'Don't you agree?' she prompts and her stare is unflinching. 'I mean, if you're going to use our child as a way to hurt my brother then I don't care what I promised you, I won't marry you, end of story.'

My God. Why did I ever think she was an easy mark? Easy prey for me to feast on? She's nothing but iron all the way through.

She will be an excellent mother for your child.

The thought winds through me, making the beast in me growl with approval at her strength. Because yes, she's standing up to me and challenging me, and that can only mean double the protection for our baby.

She and I will make a formidable team.

I decide there's no reason to prevaricate over this promise, since the only step I have to take to set my plan in motion is to marry her. Those vows will ensure that my child is heir to Vulcan Energy. Of course, it could be that Ulysses might have children of his own at some point, but I can reassess when the time comes.

'I won't ever use our child,' I say and I realise that even as the words come out of my mouth, I mean it. In fact, I've never meant anything more in my entire life. 'I give you my word.'

She stares at me a moment longer, then she nods. 'Okay, good. So, back to the subject of being your wife. How exactly is that going to work?'

CHAPTER TWELVE

Olympia

HE'S LYING BACK against the headboard of the bed, his muscular arms folded across the hard expanse of his chest, his dark eyes enigmatic, giving nothing away.

I knew he would come back to what I told him, about the things I've been through. I didn't make the mistake of thinking he'd forgotten. And while I didn't actually want to tell him, I knew he wouldn't let it go until I had.

So I told him about my foster parents and what they did to me and saw the anger ignite in his eyes. It wasn't at me, I knew that too, but I didn't want his anger. I appreciated that he felt it on my behalf, but I didn't want to have to reassure him the way I had to with Ulysses. Not that Ulysses needed reassuring, but the way he fashioned his whole life to revolve around me and watching him martyr himself to the guilt of leaving me in an abusive situation was exhausting. I was tired of being his Rapunzel and I certainly wasn't going to be Rafael's.

Rafael understood though, I had to give him that. But then he spoiled it by telling me that I was his responsibility, which I didn't appreciate one bit. Then again, he also pointed out that he wasn't Ulysses and that he wasn't going to keep me tucked away like a delicate hothouse flower. He was very emphatic about that and about not using our child as a way to get his revenge.

I'm doubtful of his promises, especially given his fury at what Ulysses did to his family, but the fierce look in his eyes when he said he wouldn't use the baby makes me want to believe in that promise at least.

I'm still tense though. I need to know what being his wife will mean for me and I'm not going to agree to the marriage until I do. Yes, I know that I made him a promise, but if he thinks he'll keep me in the house like a good little wife, he's got another think coming.

'How being my wife will work, you mean?' he asks.

'Yes. I want to know what you were thinking when you demanded I marry you.'

A muscle flicks in his hard jaw. He's annoyed. I'm pushing him and I suspect he's not a man who's ever been pushed. Too bad though. I've learned a few things being Ulysses's sister and one of those things is how to drive a hard bargain with a stubborn, difficult man.

'Very well,' he says flatly. 'If you want the truth, I didn't think about it.'

I'm unsurprised. Of course he didn't think about it, because he was too busy thinking what a perfect revenge it was going to make. 'Then I suggest you start,' I snap. 'Because a wife and a child aren't just for Christmas, Rafael. They're for ever.'

Temper gleams in his eyes and again I feel the addictive rush of power that I've managed to affect him this way. He has a line, I'm sure he does, and I want to know where it is. Though, really, I shouldn't be pushing him for the sake of it. I do have my reasons and I'm certainly not going to exchange one prison for another. This isn't just about me, either. It's about our child and what kind of life we'll have as a family, because, like it or not, we *will* be a family. And I want that family to be a close and loving one, so our child will grow up feeling safe and loved. I want him or her to have the kind of childhood that I never did.

'Fine,' Rafael says, an edge in his deep voice. 'I don't want an on-paper-only marriage, or for my wife and child to live apart from me.'

'So you want me and the child to live here?'

'Yes.' His eyes blaze. 'I grew up in this house and this is my home. It will become our child's and yours too.'

I like that there's a family history here and that he wants to continue it. And I don't mind that it's not in Greece, where I grew up. The house in Athens was never mine, it was always Ulysses's, and I was constantly weighed down there by my sense of obligation towards him. I feel no such obligation towards Rafael, however, and even though this house isn't mine either, at least it could represent the start of something new and different and exciting.

Still, I don't want to give away that I like this idea, because I don't want to give away any advantage, so I only nod. 'I see. I live here and warm your bed presumably.'

His onyx eyes narrow. 'It won't be "my" bed, Olympia. It will be "our" bed. And yes, I expect you to sleep with me every night. I expect you to be my wife in every way.'

A delicious shiver runs through me, because, yet again, I like that idea too. Of being his wife, sleeping in his bed, sleeping with him. 'And I suppose you'll expect me to be faithful too,' I say, aiming for casual.

Instantly his ready temper ignites and he leans forward, reaching for me, his fingers wrapping around my upper arms as he hauls me up and onto his hard, hot chest. 'Yes,' he growls. 'I expect you to be faithful. If you even so much as touch—'

'You will be faithful too,' I demand, cutting him off, secretly thrilling to the firmness of his grip and the possessive glitter in his eyes. 'What goes for me, goes for you also.'

'Done,' he says, far too quickly. 'After this hunger wears off we can renegotiate, but until then, the only bed we share will be this one.'

I take a silent, shaken breath, trying not to be so conscious of how his bare skin is against mine and it's hot, and he's hard. Very, very hard. 'I will have my own life too,' I say, continuing to push. 'You won't interfere with anything I choose to do and the same will go for me. I won't interfere with anything you do.'

His gaze drops to my mouth and back up again. He's as affected by my closeness as I am by his. 'But any decisions we make on behalf of our child we will make together. I will be a part of his or her life, dragonfly. I won't be sidelined, understand?'

Again that thrill pulses through me at the certainty in his eyes. At the conviction glowing there, as well as the determination. Our child has become real to him now and he wants to be a father, and I can't help but love that. Our baby will have what I never did: parents determined to do the best for them no matter what.

'I understand,' I say, unable to keep the husk from my voice.

'Good.' He keeps on staring at me, searching my face. 'So now it's your turn. You want your own life and I've agreed. What else do you need?'

Surprise ripples through me. I didn't expect him to ask me what I want and I very much like that he has. Though, like him, it's not something I've given much thought to. It's difficult to think with him looking at me that way, but I force my straying thoughts back on track. 'I…want something of my own. My own space,' I manage. 'Not just a room, but maybe a…little studio or something. Separate from the villa.'

His eyes widen slightly. 'A studio? For what?'

I feel self-conscious all of a sudden, though there really isn't any reason for it, and so I force myself to say, 'I want to do something. I want a purpose. Ulysses was planning on giving me a position at Vulcan Energy, but the last thing I want is a job in someone else's company, especially my brother's.'

'You want a career?' he asks, his intense gaze boring a hole through my forehead.

'Yes.' I'm irritated with myself and how self-conscious I feel as I say the words. 'I want a job. I want to earn my own money. I want a life that's mine for a change, and not a monument to Ulysses's guilt.'

'Why does he feel so guilty about you?'

I let out a breath. 'Because after my mother died, he promised that we'd stay together. That we wouldn't be sent to different homes, but he was wrong and we were. He was too young to get me away from my foster parents and it took him a couple of years to get together the resources to do it. So...he blames himself that it took him that long and that I had to live in such a terrible situation the whole time.'

'And do you blame him?' Rafael asks. The look in his eyes is ferocious, but there is no accusation in his voice.

'No,' I say truthfully. 'Of course, I don't, and he knows that. It's why this whole thing with him is impossible.'

'Why? Because he's making it all about him?'

I stare at him a moment, pleased with the observation. 'Yes, that's exactly it. It's all about him and his failings, yet I'm the one having to deal with the consequences and it's frustrating.'

Rafael says nothing, but the ferocity in his eyes doesn't lessen. 'I can see that. So, what kind of job do you want?'

'I'm not sure yet. I was going to take a jewellery-making course because I like the idea of creating pretty things.' I say this last with a hint of challenge, half of me afraid that this little idea of mine is too narrow or too paltry to be worth pursuing, but he only nods.

'I can build you a studio,' he says. 'There's plenty

of room here on the property. If you want it here, of course.'

There's a warmth inside me, one that grows and deepens as he speaks, because he's greeting my confession with absolute seriousness and I appreciate that a lot. Not that Ulysses was ever dismissive of what I wanted, but I could tell that was only because what I wanted fitted in well with his own plans.

For a moment I consider having a studio built somewhere else, but then drop the idea. If Rafael is here and our child is here, then definitely I want to be here too. 'Yes,' I say. 'That would be wonderful.' And just like that the hard line of his mouth relaxes.

'Good,' he says. 'You and I will sit down and discuss what you want, then I'll draw up some plans for you.'

The way his eyes glitter and his mouth curves slightly, as if the idea of building me a studio pleases him too, makes my chest tighten. I like how my request isn't a drama, too, and doesn't involve endless negotiation. He just agreed as if it was no trouble.

Eventually you'll end up being trouble. You always do.

I shove that thought out of my head since it has no business being there. Ulysses martyred himself to his own guilt and I won't do the same with mine. I just won't. It's there, I know it is. Guilt that my brother's life ended up revolving around me. Guilt that I caused him so much pain, even though I know it wasn't my fault. But I can't dwell on that and I won't let it stop me from doing what I want with Rafael. And right now, what I want is him.

I move, sliding my body on top of his, straddling

his lean hips and putting my palms on his hard chest to push myself up, so he's the one looking up at me for a change. His black eyes glitter as his gaze lowers to my bare breasts. My nipples are tight and hard, and I can feel him get even harder, his cock pressing between my thighs, making my breath catch.

'Is there something else you want?' He raises his gaze to meet mine and his beautiful mouth curves in a smug, arrogant smile.

'Maybe.' I shift on him, moving my hips, sliding against him, and have the satisfaction of seeing fire blaze high in his dark eyes.

'Ask for it,' he says, his gaze unflinching. 'Ask me nicely.'

My God, the things he can do to me just by looking at me. 'Fuck me, Rafael,' I breathe. 'Please.'

He smiles and pulls me down.

CHAPTER THIRTEEN

Rafael

GETTING DELIVERIES ON Christmas Day is difficult, but nothing is too much trouble when you have money and today I spend mine like water.

After another few incredible hours in bed, I leave Olympia sleeping. I can't lie there when there's work to be done and certainly not after that conversation. I'm strangely energised at the thought of preparing things for her, especially when it comes to making things legal between us. I want that to happen as soon as possible, especially with her brother knowing where she is. He might decide to come after her immediately, regardless of how she told him not to, and if so, I want us to be married before he arrives. Again, getting a priest and a witness is difficult on Christmas Day, but I have favours I can call in—Sicily is a small place in many ways and plenty of people owe me. Tomorrow will be the day we tie the knot.

It takes only a couple of hours to organise the things that I need for the marriage to take place, then I go into my office at the back of the house, grab a blank sheet of paper and a pencil and sit at my desk to start sketching the bare bones of the little studio she wants.

It's been a long time since I've done any drawing. I used to when I was a boy, finding a simple pleasure in sketching. I like the tactile feel of a pencil and paper rather than a tablet, and buildings are a favourite of mine to draw. Before my father died, I wanted to be an architect, but he didn't approve. He wanted me to work in the family business and all I wanted was to make him happy, make him proud, so I did what I was told. Afterwards…well, there was no time for drawing. I had to earn money and fast, and being an enforcer for one of the local *Cosa Nostra* families was the only way to do it.

Now, though, it feels good to hold a pencil in my hand. To draw straight, bold lines across a crisp, clean sheet of paper, and curved lines too, because my dragonfly is not only bold, but she has curves and arcs too. Her little studio needs to encapsulate the iron of her spirit, yet not only the iron. There's a softness to her, too, an essential femininity that makes my breath catch and sends all the blood to my groin, and that needs to be there as well.

I lose myself in the pleasure of sketching and I'm not sure how long I sit there, but suddenly there's a touch on my shoulder and a soft, sweet scent, the brush of silky hair over my arm, and I realise that Olympia has come up behind me and is leaning over me, staring at the sketch.

I have a strange urge to cover the drawing, to hide it from her until I'm ready for her to see it, because it's not done. But I resist the urge. It's childish and, besides, does it matter what she thinks? I can always change it anyway.

'What's this?' she asks, her voice close to my ear.

Even after the hours spent in bed, her physical presence distracts me, so it takes me a minute to answer. 'Your studio,' I say. 'I had an idea for it so I thought I'd do a quick sketch to see what you think.'

I push my chair to the side to give her room, glancing at her face as she leans down to get a closer look. She must have gone through one of my drawers because she's wearing one of my T-shirts and seeing her in it makes me suddenly ravenous. Before I can think, I reach for her, pulling her down into my lap, her warmth and gentle weight soothing for reasons I can't explain.

She doesn't resist, settling back against me as if she's been sitting in my lap for years and it's as natural for her as breathing. 'This is wonderful, Rafael,' she murmurs, staring at my sketch. There's wonder in her voice and I can't stop the boyish pride that rushes through me. 'You can really draw.'

I don't want to give away how much her pleasure means to me, so all I say is, 'I used to when I was a child.'

It comes out much gruffer than I intended and she turns her head, glancing up at me. 'You don't any more?'

'No. I'm a CEO. Not much time for drawing when you're managing a huge company.'

'Well, it's amazing.' She glances back at the drawing. 'I love all the windows and the little porch out the front.' She touches the roofline where I've drawn in some skylights. 'Will it face the sea?'

'Yes. There's a place on the edge of the cliff overlooking the ocean where this would be perfect.' I pause, looking at her face. She's still staring at the sketch, but all I can see are the elegant lines of her cheekbone and nose, the soft curves of her lips. My chest tightens for reasons I can't explain. 'If the sea reminds you too much of Athens, we can build it somewhere else.'

'No,' she says, still looking at the building I've drawn for her. 'No, this is absolutely perfect.'

I shouldn't care what she thinks of this sketch. It shouldn't matter at all, yet I'm savagely pleased with the wonder in her voice. With the way she's tracing the lines of the drawing as if she's never seen such an amazing thing in all her life.

Perfect, she said. It's perfect.

She's perfect.

I slide my arms around her, holding her close. 'Is this what you'd like me to build for you?'

'Yes,' she says emphatically and then twists around to look at me. Her golden eyes are glowing, her cheeks pink with pleasure. 'This is exactly what I want, Rafael. The sea and the light...it's perfect. How did you know?'

'You said you wanted to make jewellery, which means you need light. And again, the sea means something to you, I think. I also thought you'd like it to be set away from the main house so you could feel as if you're really in your own space.'

'Yes.' Her mouth curves in the most beautiful smile. 'Yes, it's all exactly right.' She turns back to look at the sketch again. 'Your drawing is so good. You should do more of it.'

'I used to love drawing buildings,' I say, not sure why I'm even telling her this and yet unable to stop. 'I had a sketchbook I used to carry around with me. I actually wanted to be an architect.'

'Oh, did you?' This time, she leans back in my arms, her head resting on my shoulder, looking up at me again. 'You didn't pursue it?'

'No. My father wanted me to work in the family business and I wanted to please him, so that's what I did. And then...' I stop.

'And then Ulysses took your family's business,' she continues for me, her gaze enigmatic. 'What about after that?'

I don't want to get into this, but it's not as if I haven't told her. 'You know what happened after that. I already said. I worked for the *consiglieri* of one of the *Cosa Nostra* families.'

She blinks. 'So, the Mafia, then.'

'Yes.' I give her a thin smile. 'I wasn't much interested in architecture after that.'

'Why not?'

The question discomforts me for reasons I can't articulate. 'Why draw when you can hire someone to draw for you?' I say casually. 'I have an entire department of architects now. I don't need to do it myself.'

'And yet you enjoyed drawing this. I know you did.'

She's not wrong, but I don't like her saying so. 'Yes, I did. But why should my enjoyment matter?'

'Because you're uncomfortable with me pointing

it out,' she shoots back. 'Why is that? Does it remind you of your family?'

'Why do you care?' I turn the question back on her.

'I'm going to be your wife, Rafael,' she says without hesitation. 'Shouldn't I care?'

She's so close, her scent and warmth distracting me and making it difficult for me to think. And I need to think. Especially if we're going to be having this conversation. 'No,' I say and gently ease her from my lap. 'You shouldn't.' I push back my chair and stand. 'Don't waste any emotion on me, dragonfly. That's one thing I won't require of you.'

She leans against the desk and frowns. 'What do you mean?'

'I mean, you don't have to care about me.'

'But aren't I supposed to care? In sickness and in health, I thought.'

'That's not the kind of marriage we'll be having,' I say, my voice flat. 'Certainly it will be physical and obviously there will be respect between us, but nothing more.'

Her frown deepens. 'I know we're not in love right now,' she says with such blunt honesty that I'm taken aback. 'I mean, we barely know each other. But surely after some time has passed and we—'

'No.' I can't help myself interrupting. 'There will be nothing more between us, Olympia. I can't do love. I won't, understand?'

Something in her gaze flickers. 'Why not?'

I can't tell if there's a deeper meaning in her question, but I can't lie to her. I can give her only the truth.

'Because love is not something I'm prepared to give anyone.'

Her expression doesn't change. 'That doesn't answer my question.'

'Love didn't save my father,' I say, unable to stop the bitterness from leaking into my voice. 'I loved him very much, but in the end it didn't mean anything to him. I know it didn't, because if it did, he wouldn't have taken his own life.'

Again, something flickers across her face, and I have a horrible feeling it's sympathy. 'Rafael...' she murmurs.

But I don't need sympathy from her. I don't need it from anyone. What happened to my father was years ago and I've long since got past it.

'I loved my father,' I repeat, pressing my point home. 'And all I wanted was to make him proud. But that wasn't enough to save him and it only ended up devastating me, so I'm not doing that again. Not ever.'

Her eyes darken. 'What about our child? Surely, you'll love them?'

There's an odd tension in me and I'm not sure why. Possibly it's because discussing this is forcing me to revisit memories I never wanted to revisit, making me re-examine choices I've already made. Since my parents died, love has never been part of my life and I've never wanted it to be. I haven't had any reason to regret that decision and I don't regret it now. But she's forcing me to look at that choice again, and I can't brush it off, not when it's about our baby.

'Yes,' I say carefully. 'I will love our child. But to be very clear, that's not something I have a choice about.'

She stares at me silently for a long moment. 'So... loving someone else is a choice?'

'Yes.' I hold her gaze. 'And if that's something you want our marriage to have then you're going to be disappointed.'

'What about me? Don't I get a say in that?'

I fold my arms. 'You want love, dragonfly? Is that what you're after?'

It's not a question I want to ask, because I don't know what I'll do if she says she does. But just when the silence becomes too long, she lifts a shoulder and glances back down at the drawing. 'No, of course not,' she says. 'I mean, I will at some point. But I don't need it from you.'

Instantly the tension in me pulls tight. Because now all I can think about is who she would get it from and where. 'You won't get it from anyone while you're married to me,' I say through clenched teeth. 'We're staying faithful to each other, remember?'

Her pretty mouth hardens and I'm regretting that the warmth and closeness of five minutes before is already evaporating under the weight of this conversation. I don't want her angry and I don't want this tension between us. Not on Christmas Day, for God's sake.

Making an effort to push aside my temper, I let out a breath, drop my arms and then hold out a hand. 'Let's not fight now, dragonfly. I have a few nice things prepared for this evening, and then tomorrow, we'll marry.'

Surprise chases the golden sparks of temper from her eyes. 'Tomorrow? Are you serious?'

'Very,' I confirm. 'I'm an impatient man and the sooner we're married, the better.'

'Better for who?' she asks, her gaze narrowing the way it often does when I say something she doesn't like. 'For you or me?'

'For both of us.' I still have my hand extended in her direction, waiting for her to take it. 'You promised me, remember?'

For a second I think she won't let me drop the subject, but then she sighs and reaches for my hand, her slender fingers threading through mine. 'Yes, I suppose so. But I'm just warning you that the nice things you've prepared for tonight better be damn nice, otherwise there'll be a riot.'

CHAPTER FOURTEEN

Olympia

I can't get what Rafael said about love out of my head. My thoughts circle around and around it, even as we settle to eat the Christmas dinner Rafael has prepared with his own hands. There is turkey and stuffing, and mashed potatoes and all sorts of other delicious side-dishes, and yet all I can think about is that he doesn't want love. That he'll love our child, but he won't love me, and he was very clear about it.

I brushed it off, of course, telling myself that the disappointment I felt when he said that didn't mean anything. That a marriage to him without love is perfectly fine. After all, he's going to build me that beautiful studio he drew and he's said that there are other nice surprises on the way, so there's no point dwelling on it, and why ruin a perfectly lovely Christmas night arguing about love? Also, his reasons for not wanting anything to do with love make sense. It must have been horrific to lose his father in that way so no wonder he doesn't want to put himself through it again.

I'm still telling myself that as we finish our Christmas dinner, then I'm distracted by what sounds like a helicopter. Rafael's expression abruptly lightens. 'Wait here,' he says, then gets up from the dinner table and strides out of the room.

I'm tense, a little worried that the helicopter might be Ulysses making a desperate rescue bid. Then again, I told him not to come for me and hopefully he listened, and the helicopter currently touching down on the lawn outside the villa is here for other reasons.

Indeed, not ten minutes later, I hear Rafael come back inside, his deep voice issuing instructions to someone. Then the front door closes and there is silence.

I'm standing by the Christmas tree and looking at all the decorations on it, some of which appear to be handmade, when he strides suddenly into the living area, his arms full of bags and boxes.

I stare at him, open-mouthed, as he puts what he's carrying down, then goes back out again, returning with yet more bags. He does this a couple more times until the whole living room is full of boxes and bags emblazoned with logos from various extremely expensive clothing labels, not to mention jewellery and make-up brands.

Rafael points to the rug in front of the fire. 'Sit down, dragonfly. I have some gifts for you.'

'So I see,' I say, staring at the vast array cluttering the floor. 'When did you get all of this?'

'Last night.' He fusses around with the boxes to clear a space for me. 'After we left Athens. I wanted to make sure you have everything you need.'

'That's an understatement,' I murmur then fall silent, not knowing what else to say. There are so many presents, but I have nothing to give him, nothing at all, and I don't like that. It feels one-sided. As if I'm still a poor, abused victim who can never be asked for anything because I'm too fragile and too broken to have any kind of demand placed on her.

'Sit,' he urges insistently.

Part of me doesn't want to sit, let alone accept all of these gifts, but he's obviously gone to so much trouble, I can't refuse. 'When you said you'd ordered me a whole wardrobe, you weren't kidding,' I say as I sit down in the one clear spot in front of the fire.

'If it was up to me,' he says, picking up a large white box and handing it to me, 'you'd wear nothing at all.'

'Good thing it's not up to you, then.' I take the box from him and he sits on the couch, watching me as I open it.

Inside is the loveliest gown I've ever seen. It's of rich scarlet silk with lots of trailing draperies and I already know it's going to be the perfect size when I put it on.

'I thought you could wear that tomorrow,' Rafael murmurs, his gaze dark and intent. 'For our wedding.'

Ah, yes. The quickie wedding he mentioned earlier. I wanted to argue with him about the speed of it, but it was clear he'd made up his mind and wouldn't be moved. So I dropped the subject. He said he didn't want to fight and I realised I didn't want to either.

Now, looking at this beautiful gown, I'm reminded again of it. 'Tomorrow,' I echo, looking at him.

'Yes.' There's a steely edge in his voice.

Don't argue with him, not now, not when you're surrounded by all the gifts he got you. Anyway, what does it matter when you get married?

It doesn't matter, not in the end. And after all, I did promise him. Still, I feel a little railroaded. It reminds me of the times Ulysses would get me things or do things for me and, while they were always nice things, I would always feel a little annoyed by them, mainly because he would never ask my opinion about whether I wanted them or not. And also because I knew he was getting them for me out of guilt.

Naturally, I'd then feel bad for being annoyed, because it wasn't as if he was being awful. He was just trying to be good to me and, really, I should be grateful for all that he did for me.

Those complicated, messy feelings hit me again, though it's different with Rafael. He is the one who kidnapped me, so I don't have to feel bad for feeling annoyed. And I can say things to him that I'd never say to Ulysses, because Rafael isn't eaten up with guilt in the same way my brother is. In fact, Rafael was using me as a chess piece in his little game of revenge, so, really, I can say anything I like to him and I don't have to feel bad in any way.

'I hope you're not expecting me to be grateful for all of this,' I say bluntly.

'No,' he answers without hesitation. 'Why would I expect that? I'm the one who kidnapped you.'

'But you want me to be grateful for this wedding gown, for the wedding you organised, that you'll force me to take part in.'

His eyes narrow. 'I didn't force you, Olympia. You promised.'

'You bought me this dress. And you want me to wear it—'

'I don't give a shit about the dress,' he interrupts sharply. 'I got it for you so you'd have something pretty to wear, but if you don't want to wear it, I'll marry you wearing nothing at all.'

My heart is beating fast, the complicated mix of emotions roiling inside me. I'm not sure why I'm challenging him now. Maybe it's just because I can, because he's not Ulysses and I don't have to be careful of his feelings the way I am with my brother's.

A silence falls. I don't want to apologise, but I also don't want to spoil the evening with my own bad temper.

'What is this all about, dragonfly?' Rafael asks after a moment, his expression one of genuine puzzlement. 'Is it the wedding? Or is it all the gifts? I got them all for you, but if you don't like them, I can ship them all back. I won't lose sleep over it.'

I let out a breath, and give him the truth. 'My brother used to shower me with clothes and toys and...all kinds of things. And they were always nice things, but... I never wanted them and I didn't ask for them, and I knew he was only getting them for me because of his guilt. They weren't for *me*, if that makes sense.'

Rafael watches me, his dark gaze enigmatic. 'And you didn't like them?'

'No, it wasn't that. I did like them. But... I felt I couldn't tell him even if I didn't like them, because it would hurt him. I just hated that he felt guilty because of me and so I tried to be grateful, even when I wasn't.'

There's a long silence, then Rafael says very clearly, 'Don't ever feel that you have to be grateful with me, Olympia. I don't want a facade. I want honesty.'

He really means that, I can see, and something tight inside me relaxes. 'You want me to like this dress, though, don't you?' I say, only slightly teasing.

He smiles, making me feel warm all over. 'Yes. I do. But if you don't, that's okay.'

Another thing he really means, and I can't help but smile back, my bad temper fading. 'I don't like it,' I tell him. 'I love it. It's beautiful.'

His smile deepens and that's beautiful too. 'Here,' he says, picking up another box and handing it to me. 'These go with it.'

I open it and there are some high-heeled red silk sandals, with red soles, and I love those too. My throat closes. 'How did you know these would be so perfect?' I ask. 'And that I'd love them?'

'I didn't know,' he admits. 'I just thought of that night in Singapore, when we met, and how beautiful you were in red.'

It's simple praise, but I glow all the same. I can't help it. I love it when he calls me beautiful.

I open more boxes and bags, loving how each one isn't the kind of gift I'd get from Ulysses. Those were gifts to his sister, but none of these are sisterly in the slightest. They're not for the girl I never had a chance of being or the broken teenager reverting to childhood for safety. They're gifts for a woman. Silky underwear in a rainbow of colours, sexy bras, negligees and knickers. A couple of other gowns, one of emerald silk, with a high leg slit, and another of black, with a plunging neckline. Skimpy bikinis that barely cover anything. And that's not all. There are form-fitting dresses, practical jeans and tees, and soft cashmere sweaters. There are also other shoes, both sexy high heels and sneakers, and then boxes and boxes of make-up and toiletries, all high-end and all extremely expensive.

I love them all. They're pretty, all to my taste, pregnancy-friendly, and I just know they're all going to fit. And indeed, when he asks me to model them for him, they do fit, and superbly.

I waft around in the emerald-green gown, turning in front of him as he sits on the couch, his dark eyes burning.

'Beautiful,' he murmurs. 'Dragonfly, you stop my heart.'

I give him a curtsey. 'Thank you, kind sir.'

And this time it's my heart stopping as he smiles. 'Do you like them all, then?' he asks. 'Are there any you want me to return?'

As with everything he says, he means it, and I know too that it wouldn't bother him if there were some I didn't like. But I do like them, *all* of them, and I want him to know that. So I stop wafting and come to a stop in front of him.

'I love them,' I say honestly. 'I love all of them.' Then I go on, because I want him to know this, too. 'My brother's presents were all things for a little girl, a teenager, or a sister. Not a woman.' I shift one leg to the side, allowing the green silk of the gown to slide away, the slit in the dress extending up to my hip. 'This, for example, is very definitely for a woman.'

Rafael's dark gaze drops to my thigh and his expression turns hungry. 'Good,' he says, then glances up at me again. 'Because that's what you are. A sexy, beautiful, strong woman.'

I'm not used to being looked at the way he's looking at me, but I like it. It makes me feel all of those things that he told me I am, sexy and beautiful and most of all strong. Because I want to be strong, especially after spending so many years feeling so weak.

Suddenly, I want to give him something too—I don't want to be the only one who receives—except I have nothing to give him.

His gaze sharpens as if he can read my every thought. 'What's wrong?'

'You've given me all these beautiful things. But I don't have anything to give you,' I say slowly.

'I don't need anything.' His gaze darkens, intensifies. 'I have everything I need right here.'

He means me, I know it, and abruptly, I know what to give him.

'Tell me,' I say, holding his gaze. 'Tell me what you want and I'll give it to you. Anything you want, anything at all. It'll be my Christmas gift to you.'

He stares at me, the black flames in his eyes rising higher. 'Dragonfly...'

I don't move and I don't look away. 'I want to, Rafael. Please. Ulysses never asked anything of me, because he thought I was too broken, too fragile. But...

you said I was strong and I want to be treated as if I am.' I take a step closer to where he's sitting on the couch, the green silk billowing around my legs. 'So. Tell me. What do you want for Christmas, Rafael Santangelo?'

The darkness in his eyes shifts then blazes. 'Put on some of that scarlet lipstick,' he murmurs, gesturing to the small gold box sitting by the couch.

I'm a little puzzled by the request, but I obey. There's a tiny mirror that comes with the lipstick tube, so I'm able to apply it without issue. The colour is fire-engine red and it makes my mouth look full and pouty.

'Good,' he says approvingly as I put the lipstick down. 'Now, take off your underwear, but keep the gown on.'

I reach beneath the hem and slide my knickers down my legs and then step out of them. His gaze follows every movement and once my underwear is off, he orders, 'Kneel.' And points to the spot on the rug in front of where he's sitting.

My heart beats faster, because I know what he wants now, and I'm desperate to give it to him, so I kneel in front of him.

'Undo my jeans,' he demands.

My fingers shake as I do his bidding, desire and anticipation making my mouth go dry. He's hard behind the denim and I can feel the pressure building between my own thighs in anticipation.

'Take my cock out.' His voice is deeper, almost a purr. 'Then take it in your mouth. I want to see those red lips wrapped around it.'

The hot words fall like sparks on my skin, igniting

me, and I'm breathing fast as I lean forward, reaching into his jeans. He's hot and so hard, and his skin is like silk, and when I put my hands on him, I feel the muscles in his thighs tense.

He wants this so badly, I can see it in his eyes, his expression searing as he watches. So I meet his gaze and I hold it as I open my mouth and wrap my lips around him, exactly as he wanted.

He hisses in pleasure, his hands sliding into my hair and gathering it in his fists. 'Suck me, dragonfly,' he growls. 'Make me see stars with your mouth.'

And I want to. I want to make him see stars, see God himself. Send him to heaven and back, knowing that it was me who gave him that. Me who gave him such pleasure. So I do what he tells me, tasting him, exploring him with my tongue, nipping him with my teeth, and working him with my mouth. Then I watch the savage pleasure that ripples over his face, thrilling to the intensity of it, my own pleasure building higher and higher the more he's affected by me and what I'm doing to him.

He murmurs something then, a vicious word in Italian, and I'm startled as he pulls my head away.

'What are you—?' I begin.

But he's already hauling me up into his arms, shoving the green silk of my gown out of the way as he sits me in his lap, facing him. Then he looks down at his cock and the red marks on his skin left by my lipstick, and he shifts me, spreading me open delicately, then pushing inside me in one deep stroke.

'Like this,' he says roughly as I gasp aloud. 'I want you like this.'

Then he's pulling my mouth down on his, his kiss hungry, savage almost, and definitely demanding. I answer the demand, too, because I want him to want more. I want him to demand it, to let me know he doesn't see me as fragile. That he truly believes what he says when he tells me I'm strong.

And he does. He give me no quarter and in releasing his own demanding nature, he releases mine. I kiss him back just as savagely and I'm just as demanding. I glory in how hard he grips me and in the sharp, deep thrusts of his hips. I love the feeling of his teeth against my bottom lip and then lower, against the side of my neck and then my collarbones.

He's demanding, yet he's the one slipping his hand down between my legs, his fingers on my clit, giving me the extra friction I need like a gentleman, and I'm the one who comes first, crying out his name. Seconds later, he gives one deep thrust before joining me in the flames.

CHAPTER FIFTEEN

Rafael

I HOLD HER in my arms, my head fallen back against the back of the couch, staring sightlessly up at the ceiling as the aftershocks of that incredible orgasm grip me tight.

Dio. What has she done to me? I feel emptied out, sated, peaceful almost, in a way I've never felt before, not even after that night in Singapore. Or even the sex we had earlier today, and I'm not sure why.

Is it because of how she gave herself to me? Obeying my demands without question and then matching me in passion? Or is it because of how she was honest with me before, about the gifts her brother would give her and what a pressure that became for her?

I'm not sure, and perhaps it should worry me that I can't put a finger on why, yet, right now, with her in my arms, all wrapped up in the green silk gown I knew would look amazing on her, it doesn't seem that important. I don't want to think about it now anyway. What I want is to sit here like this, with her in my arms, and not think about a single damn thing, except how lovely she looked unwrapping all the presents I gave her, and how the pleasure she took in them was mine.

It was also satisfying to know that they were different from the ones her brother got her, and that she loved that. Not that I needed her appreciation—I meant what I said when I told her I'd send them all back if she didn't like them—but I did like the pleasure she took in them.

It's been a long time since I've thought about nonsexual pleasure, but sitting on the couch watching her open all those boxes and bags, I was thinking of hers, and how strange it was to find that it was important to me.

I can't recall the last time anything but my revenge was important to me, but somehow Olympia Zakynthos's happiness has become so.

It's a strange thing to admit and not one I'm ready to confess, not yet, so I stay silent as she shifts on me, lifting her head from where it lies on my shoulder and glancing up at me. Her hair is tumbled and her lipstick smeared and she looks gloriously ravished.

'Dangerous, dragonfly,' I murmur. 'Watching you suck me was the most erotic sight I've ever seen.'

Oh,' she says, blushing. 'That's good.'

Her obvious embarrassment is charming, especially after what we've just done, but I shift, deciding we need to move to the floor and rid ourselves of our clothes. I proceed to help her take off the gown and it's like unwrapping my own, most delicious present. Then I take off the jeans and tee that I'm wearing, before I bring her down onto the soft rug in front of the fireplace.

I rain kisses all over her delectable body, wanting to give back at least some of the pleasure she gave me. She protests that I don't need to reciprocate, but I silence her with my mouth, and then my hands, and then I take her beneath me and slide into her once again, moving slow and easy. I want to draw her pleasure out for as long as I can, and this time, when the orgasm comes, it's a slow, gentle wave, cresting and cresting before rolling over us, rather than a hurricane smashing everything in its path.

Afterwards we lie in the warm, sated silence, the detritus of boxes and bags scattered everywhere, the Christmas tree glittering above us.

'Some of those decorations are handmade,' she says after a long moment, her voice soft and husky. 'Did you make them?'

'What gave it away?' I'm on my back, my arm under my head, staring up at the branches of the tree. 'The ineptly drawn reindeer or the badly applied glitter?'

She laughs. She's got her head on my chest, her black hair spilling over my skin, and we're wrapped up in a soft cashmere blanket. 'All of the above?' Her voice is warm with humour. 'Seriously, though. You made them, did you?'

'I did.' I stare up at them and allow myself the memory. 'I did those ones at school. And then I would save a bit of pocket money to buy new ones for the tree every year. My mother loved them. We would hang them up together every Christmas.'

The memories, surprisingly, aren't as painful as they have been. Perhaps it's time. Or perhaps it's Olympia's warm body pressed close to mine that makes it feel as if the pain has drained from them.

'I'm so sorry about your parents,' Olympia murmurs after a long moment. 'That must have been really hard.'

In this moment it feels easy to talk with her. 'It was,' I say. 'My mother died of cancer a couple of years after Dad.'

'Oh,' she breathes. 'That's awful.'

'Yes,' I agree, because it was awful. 'I do have lots of lovely memories of her though.'

'I don't remember mine,' she says. 'She died when I was very young. And I never knew my father. You're lucky to have memories.'

I stare up into the branches of the tree, remembering other things. My simple childish thought that I could take on extra work after school to help pay the family debt. The way my father shouted at me that it would take a lifetime to repay, not a paltry few euros from a paper round. The blood in his study, on the carpet and the wall behind his chair. The way I made no difference to him, none at all.

But all I say is, 'In some ways.' I don't want to bring the subject of my father up and all the bitterness that brings with it.

'Ulysses always gave me a Christmas ornament,' she says, giving me the grace of a change of subject. 'And I'm a little sad I won't get to see what he bought me this Christmas.'

I glance down at her, conscious once again of what I've taken her from. 'I'll buy you one,' I tell her.

She's smiling, though. 'Don't you dare. Not after

you practically buried me in gifts.' Her smile fades a little. 'But you have to let me give too.'

'What do you mean?'

'Ulysses never made any demands of me. Never had any expectations, either. Initially, that was what I needed, but…after a while, it started to make me feel as if I was still broken.'

The Christmas-tree lights cast colours over her lovely face and all I can think is that there is nothing broken about her. 'In what way?' I ask, curious.

'Oh, well, I told you he cosseted and coddled me. I didn't have to give him birthday presents or make time for him. He didn't expect me to get good marks at school either or have ambitions for a career.'

I remember my father and his own expectations of me, which were high. 'Some people might find that reassuring,' I say.

'I know,' she admits. 'And like I said, I liked that at first. But after a while, I started asking myself why he didn't want anything from me or even have hopes for me. It was as if he thought I'd never get over what happened to me and I'd be destined to live as a recluse in his house for ever.'

I study her face, her lovely golden eyes, and I can see how that would frustrate her. She has a passionate, fiery spirit, desperate for some kind of outlet, and yet her brother stifled it. He suffocated her with kindness, no matter that it was well meaning.

'And do you want me to place demands on you?' I ask. 'Have expectations of you?'

'As if you haven't had demands and expectations already,' she says, a glint of humour in her eyes. 'I like it, though. So yes, I want them.'

I shift, easing her off my chest and rolling onto my side, propping my head up on one hand so I can look down into her face. 'Why?' I ask, curious as to why she likes it.

'Because it's as if you just assume that I'm as strong as you, as if that's not in any doubt, and so... I am.' She runs light fingers down my side, making my skin tighten. 'Your demands show you care, too. In fact, I think you care very deeply.'

I'm uncomfortable with that observation, yet instead of changing the subject, I find myself asking, 'So, being demanding equals care?'

'Well, doesn't it? I mean, you didn't kidnap me for nothing. You kidnapped me to hurt my brother, to gain revenge for your parents. Because they died and you loved them.'

My heart tightens, no matter how I ignore it, and I get the sudden feeling that she can see right through me. That her golden eyes can read my every thought. It's uncomfortable to be so vulnerable and extremely unfamiliar and I don't like it one bit.

It's true though, isn't it? You loved them and, in the end, that love mattered not at all.

'Rafael?' She's frowning at me, as if something in my face has given me away. 'What's wrong?'

I want to change the subject, yet the way she's touching me, her fingers tracing patterns on my skin, seems to draw the words from me even though I don't want to say them. 'I loved them, it's true,' I say. 'And I had an idyllic childhood in many ways, but...'

Her dark brows draw together. 'But what?'

Anger flickers to life inside me, a steady, burning flame. 'My father killed himself.' The words are blunt, harsh. 'So what did it matter that I loved him? He certainly didn't care.'

Concern flickers in her eyes, but I don't want to see it. I already feel as if she's turned me inside out, and that doesn't help. I glance away, reaching out to trace a lazy circle around her hip.

'I'm sure he loved you,' she says quietly. 'There are lots of reasons why people take their own lives.'

'He was a coward.' My voice is bitter and some part of me feels like a traitor for even saying it. 'If he loved me and my mother, he'd never have done it.'

The concern in her eyes deepens and there is a terrible kind of pity there, too. 'It's not your fault, Rafael,' she says softly. 'Who knows why he did what he did, but it wasn't anything to do with you.'

'I know it's not about me,' I snarl, vulnerability and bitterness making me vicious. 'But I had to deal with the consequences all the same.'

This time, it's her who moves. She sits up and reaches for me, taking my face between her palms, the look in her eyes cutting me to the bone. 'I know,' she says forcefully, her iron will showing in her voice. 'Believe me, I know what it's like having to bear consequences. We should never have had to deal with them, but we did, and it's not right and it's not fair. But...it's okay to love him, Rafael. It's okay to love him even though he hurt you.'

'I don't need your permission,' I can't help growling. 'Anyway, I stopped loving him years ago.'

But she stares at me unflinching. 'It doesn't mean forgiveness. It's just acknowledging what's already there.'

I want to demand what the point of that is, but the sympathy and concern in her voice stop me. Anger is a poor reward for her and she deserves better than that.

So I grip her wrists gently and pull her hands from my face, before pulling her down onto the rug next to me. 'Dragonfly,' I murmur as I kiss her beautiful mouth. 'I don't want to talk about this any more.'

And I move over her, making sure we don't speak of it again for the rest of the night.

CHAPTER SIXTEEN

Olympia

THE NEXT MORNING I stand in Rafael's bedroom, gazing at my reflection in the full-length mirror, and am pleased with myself. The beautiful scarlet gown he bought me fits to perfection, hugging my curves and accentuating the slight bump of my pregnancy. And I've just spent a happy half an hour playing with all my new make-up. I've put on the red lipstick. I know how much he likes it.

We're getting married this morning and there's a tight ball of nerves sitting in my stomach. I can't stop thinking about what he told me last night, about his parents, about how much he loved them, and about the anger in his voice when he called his father a coward.

My heart hurt for him then, for his anger and for the pain of the love he so clearly still feels, no matter what he said. I only wanted him to know that it's okay to be angry, but it's also okay to still love someone who hurt you. It doesn't mean you forgive them for what they did, it's merely an acknowledgement of what's in your heart. You can love someone and be furious with them, and that's difficult.

I didn't have his losses, not in the same way. Yes, I lost my mother, but I can barely remember her. I never knew my father, and my only experience of a family involved blood and pain. But that flammable, complicated mix of anger and love is what I feel for my brother, and I know how it can eat away at you, burn you. No wonder Rafael's so fierce and intense, if he's got that kind of rocket fuel driving him.

'You look beautiful,' Rafael's deep voice says from the doorway, interrupting my reverie.

I turn and then have to catch my breath. He's standing there, framed by the doorway, dressed in a black suit, a white shirt and a red silk tie the exact colour of my gown. He looks dark and dangerous, and so delicious I want to eat him alive.

'So do you,' I say, because it's true.

He gives me a hungry smile, his gaze following the line of my body all the way down to my feet and then back up again. Then he moves, coming into the room and over to where I'm standing. He's holding a box in his hand. 'You're missing one thing,' he says.

'Not another box,' I say.

'Yes. And I'm not apologising for it.' His gaze glitters as he takes the top off the box.

All the air rushes from my lungs as I look to see what's inside.

Nestled in layers of tissue is the most incredible-looking jewelled dragonfly. It's nothing like the cheap ones I bought back in Singapore. This is all delicate platinum, mother of pearl, emeralds, rubies, sapphires…

Discarding the box, Rafael gently lifts it from the tissue and slides it into my hair, his touch gentle. His dark gaze is ferocious. 'There,' he murmurs. 'Now you're absolutely perfect.'

For the second time since I've been here, I feel my eyes prickle with unexpected tears, my chest tight. This marriage is only for our child, I know that, and yet this dragonfly hair clip is deeply personal. It's about us, about the pet name he calls me ever since Singapore, and for a moment I get a flash of what our marriage could be if this gift actually meant something, if we were really in love with each other. He burns so bright, this fierce, intense man, and being loved by him would be…

Don't go there. Because he won't give it to you.

I look away abruptly, unable to hold his gaze any longer, pretending to admire the clip in the mirror. 'Thank you,' I murmur, glancing at him in the glass. 'It's beautiful, Rafael.'

If he noticed my tears, he gives no sign. 'Not as beautiful as you.'

I want to tell him it's the world's corniest line, but I can't because it doesn't feel corny in this moment. He's not smiling, he's staring at me with such intensity I feel as if I'm going to spontaneously combust right there and then. I need to break the tension somehow, so I look away, examine my lipstick one last time, then say breezily, 'Is it time?'

'It is.' He extends a hand. 'Come, dragonfly.'

I take it and a sudden rush of apprehension fills me, yet his hand is warm, his fingers strong and somehow reassuring. Still, as he leads me from the bedroom and down the stairs to the living area, my heart is beating fast and hard.

I'm really marrying him, aren't I? He's going to be my husband.

My mouth dries and I swallow as I see the priest standing in front of the Christmas tree. Beside him is another man, very tall and broad, dressed in a long black, beautifully tailored overcoat. His inky hair is tinged with white at the temples, his features sharp, cruel almost, and he exudes a magnetism that just about overwhelms everything in the room.

Fear curls around my heart and, as if he somehow senses it, Rafael's fingers squeeze mine reassuringly. He says something in Italian and there is a quick discussion between him, the priest and the dangerous stranger. The stranger's eyes are pure silver as he looks at me, and Rafael says something to him that sounds like a warning. The man's mouth curls and he turns, making a gesture at the priest and saying something that I don't need to know Italian to understand. He wants to get this over and done with.

Rafael doesn't bother to introduce him and I don't ask as the priest beckons us to stand in front of him. His accent is thick, but, with Rafael's help, I manage to understand him, and am able to repeat my vows in Italian. I'm too busy thinking about my pronunciation to dwell on the ceremony itself, and before I can think straight, I find myself holding my hand out and Rafael is sliding the ring onto my finger. He obviously had that delivered yesterday too, as well as the ring he presents to me so I can put it on his finger.

Minutes later, we're husband and wife, and Rafael has pulled me close, his mouth covering mine in a hungry, possessive kiss. The stranger says something in an amused voice and Rafael lifts his head, saying something in return that makes the other man laugh.

There is some discussion afterwards and then some documents to sign, all the while Italian is spoken fast and furious around me. Then the dangerous stranger is gone and the priest with him, and I'm finally alone with my new husband.

'Who was that?' I ask as he returns to the living area after seeing them out.

'Our witness,' Rafael says. 'Vincenzo Argenti, head of the Argenti family. I worked for his *consiglieri*.'

Oh, right. 'So he's...what? The local don?'

Rafael snorts. 'If you can call the head of one of Sicily's most powerful *Cosa Nostra* families the "local don", then yes, he is.'

No wonder he looked so dangerous. 'Surely he's too important to be a random witness?'

Rafael's smile is all teeth. 'The Argenti family owed me a favour and so I decided to use it to get a priest to marry us. Then Signore Argenti thought it would be amusing to be the witness.'

There's something about that smile of his. Something...edged, savage almost, and it makes me suspicious. 'There's something you're not telling me, isn't there?'

He continues to smile like a panther with a fresh kill, feral with satisfaction. 'Your brother is on his way here.'

Shock slides like ice water down my spine. 'What?'

Rafael's eyes glitter. 'My contact in Athens notified me that he took a jet to Palermo this morning. He'll be here soon, I suspect.'

I have to catch my breath, stop my brain spinning in wild circles. Ulysses is on his way here, after I told him not to come.

Did you really think he'd listen to you?

I hoped he might, but of course he didn't. He never does. He doesn't care what I want, all that matters to him is my safety and the fact that I'm safe right here wouldn't occur to him, even when I flat out told him so.

And Rafael didn't tell you.

A sharp anger threads through the shock. I stare into his black eyes, seeing the triumph. 'You didn't tell me,' I say. 'Why not? Did you think I'd leave if I knew he was coming?'

He doesn't miss a beat. 'I don't know, would you?'

'No,' I say flatly, angry at his doubt, angry that he hasn't been honest with me. 'I promised I'd marry you and I meant it.'

'It's too late now anyway.' He gives me that same hungry smile. 'He can't take you away from me. You're his heir and now you're mine.'

I blink, my temper rising higher. 'You promised me you'd drop this revenge plan.'

'But I have.' He holds out his hands. 'Now you're

mine I don't have to do anything more. You'll inherit his company and so will I.'

I blink again, the cold feeling inside me intensifying. He didn't tell me deliberately. And he didn't listen when I told him I didn't want him to continue his revenge. He didn't listen as my brother doesn't listen. He said he wouldn't treat me the way Ulysses treats me, but he's doing that right now, isn't he? He manipulated me for his own ends and now we're married, and there's nothing I can do about it.

On cue, I hear the distant sound of a helicopter. It's getting closer.

My brother is here.

CHAPTER SEVENTEEN

Rafael

THE SOUND OF Zakynthos's helicopter is getting closer and closer, and I can't stop the intense satisfaction that curls through me.

My contact in Athens alerted me this morning that Ulysses had left and that he was bound for Palermo, which made me extremely pleased with the decision I made yesterday to call in my favour from Vincenzo Argenti. It's an old favour and he's powerful. I wasn't sure if he'd come through, but he's always been a man of his word and, sure enough, he came, bringing along his family priest.

And not before time.

Anger flickers in Olympia's golden eyes, making them glow. I knew she'd be angry that I didn't tell her this morning, but I couldn't risk it. She had to be mine before her brother got here in case he decided to take her back with him. I wanted her to be legally bound to me so that there would be no escape. She's loyal to him, she loves him and all I have on my side is that I'm the father of her child and some physical chemistry. I needed more to hold her here.

He could still take her.

He might. Or she might go with him. But now we're legally married and that's a tie that cannot easily be undone.

You should have told her he was coming, though.

She's angry, but for a second I thought I saw something like hurt flicker in her eyes. But no, it couldn't be hurt. She doesn't love me and I don't love her, so why does it matter that I didn't tell her? I did say I'd be honest with her, but I didn't lie.

A lie by omission. Also, you promised her.

I did, it's true. But I didn't actively move against Zakynthos. I merely married his sister, something I was always going to do.

Besides, I didn't want to break the fragile détente we reached last night beneath the Christmas tree. Even so, what she'd said about it being okay to love someone who hurt you stuck in my brain and I couldn't get it out. I'd spent all night thinking about it, about my father, and what he did, and how it hurt me, and how badly it hurt still, no matter how I try to deny it.

I don't want to keep thinking about it though, I want her, so I shove the thoughts aside, reaching for her instead, wanting to hold her, maybe turn her anger into desire the way I'm so good at. But she takes a step back, drawing herself up, her back straight as a board, her eyes glowing. 'You said you wouldn't treat me the way Ulysses does,' she says.

I want to close the distance between us, but I don't

move. 'And I meant it. How am I treating you like he does?'

'You didn't listen to me. I told you I wanted you to drop your revenge plan.'

'I did,' I insist. 'The wedding was always going to happen and—'

'You didn't tell me he was coming,' she snaps. 'You didn't because you wanted me married to you so he couldn't take me away.'

There's nothing I can say to that. It's the truth. 'Why does that matter?' I demand. 'I want you with me, so yes, I hurried the marriage along.'

'But don't you understand?' She stares at me as if I've changed before her eyes into someone she doesn't recognise. 'You didn't listen, and Ulysses didn't listen either. It's always about him, about his guilt, never about me or what I want. I told you that. And now you're doing the same thing. You married me to get back at him, so you can have his company. It's all about what you want, Rafael. None of it is about me.'

The force of her words slams into me like thrown stones. She's so heartbreakingly beautiful standing there, with the dragonfly I had made for her glittering in her hair. My wife.

She's right. You're not thinking about her. You're only thinking of yourself.

The sound of the helicopter is getting louder and louder. Zakynthos is nearly here. I wanted to meet him with her beside me, letting him know how completely she's mine, but Olympia takes a couple of steps towards me. 'I'll meet him,' she says forcefully, reading my mind. '*You* stay here.'

'No,' I shoot back. 'I won't allow—'

'I don't care what you'll allow,' she interrupts. 'He's *my* brother and he's here for *me*. This has got *nothing* to do with you.'

And before I can say anything, she storms past me and out of the living area. My instinct is to go after her immediately, but some lost part of me resists. It knows she's right, even though I protest the thought. This *is* about me and what I want. It's not about her, not about what she wants, and the very least I can do is let her meet her brother alone.

So I don't follow her, even though every part of me is screaming to do so. Instead, I grit my teeth and stride to the windows that overlook the lawn so I can see Olympia in her red dress, a streak of brilliant scarlet against the green grass.

I fight the need to go to her as the helicopter touches down, shoving my hands into my pockets instead, watching as the rotors slow, the door opens and a man leaps out. He's tall and powerfully built, and he moves with purpose.

Ulysses Zakynthos. The man who caused the death of my family, who stole my parents and the life we had from me.

He strides over to where she stands and my hands close into fists, the urge to go to her almost too strong for me to deny. But then he stops and I see Olympia straighten even more, drawing herself up as her brother approaches. I'm close enough to see his face and…

he looks drawn, as if he hasn't slept in years. Is that the effect taking his sister away had? Did I cause him sleepless nights? Did I cause him pain?

A savage satisfaction turns over inside me and in the glass, I see my reflection smiling viciously. Good. I hope I caused him pain because what he felt is only the faintest echo of the agony he caused me.

I can't hear what they're saying, but they're clearly having some kind of discussion. Then Olympia walks towards him and every muscle in my body tenses. I almost break and stride from the room, the urge to go outside and pull her away from him so strong I can barely resist. She can't go back with him. She can't. I won't let her.

Don't make it worse, you stupid bastard.

I grit my teeth, my jaw aching. It's true, going after her when she told me to stay here won't make things any easier between us. She's already furious with me for not listening to her and maybe she has a right to be. She promised to marry me and she did. Whereas I...

You promised to drop your revenge, but you lied.

I watch as Olympia puts her arms around her brother, hugging him, and a whisper of shame ghosts through me. It's not a feeling I'm used to, not considering how I embraced my dark side years ago, but I feel it now and I don't like it. Yet I can't escape. I promised to drop my revenge against her brother, yet I didn't, not truly. I only pushed it aside, to think about later.

What will your father think of his son now?

I know the answer to that. He'd hate what I've become. Then again, I had no choice. He was the one who decided to run away, to take himself from my mother and me in the most brutal way imaginable. I only did what I had to in order to survive.

Olympia is looking up at her brother and she's smiling, and I can see the warmth in her face and in her eyes. She loves her brother, she loves him deeply and he loves her too. And my chest hurts. It's tight and sore, and it's strange, because I don't want any part of the love they share. I don't want *her* love.

Love doesn't save you. It doesn't pay debts or keep you fed, with a roof over your head. Love is cowardice. Love is abandonment. All it does is devastate you, and I don't want any part of it.

Yet, despite that, all I can think about is what it would be like if she looked at me that way, as if she loved me, and the pain worsens.

I can't stand it, so I force myself to turn away, striding over to the drinks cabinet near the fire to pour myself a Scotch. Then I knock it back and pour myself another. The alcohol sits in my stomach, lighting a fire inside me, making me burn. Making me think about what I promised her and what I promised myself, and yes, it's true. I'm as selfish as she thinks I am. What she wanted didn't matter to me and I didn't think about that, not fully. But now I am, now I'm thinking about her strength and her determination. What she went through as a child and what I've put her through since I found out that she's carrying my child. And I think about that child, *my* child. What kind of father am I who uses his child and the mother of that child for his own ends?

I know what kind of father that is. It's the kind of father I had, who chose death, who chose his own escape, his own pain over his family.

I'm still standing there, a third Scotch in my hand, when I hear the helicopter lift off. Is she going with him? Is she choosing to leave me?

Can you blame her?

I can't blame her, that's the problem. If I was her, I'd leave me too.

My heart is wrapped in briars, thorns digging in, and I don't know why. What does it matter if she leaves? I've got what I wanted: she's my wife. She didn't ask for any kind of prenup, so what's hers is mine and what's mine is hers. Yes, she could take me for everything I have and that, out of anything, should matter to me. And yet... Is that even important if I don't have her?

I can feel someone watching me, so I turn and there she is, in the doorway, her gaze steady. A rush of the most intense relief courses through me and my hand almost shakes.

'You didn't go with him,' I say before I can stop myself.

'I thought I might,' she says, sparing me nothing. 'But I've done nothing but hide since I was ten years old, and I'm tired of it.'

Putting down my Scotch, I cross the room to where she's standing, unable to help myself. And I reach for her, pulling her to me, looking down into her golden eyes. She doesn't protest, gazing up at me steadily.

My wife. *My* wife.

'Take off your dress,' I order, the need inside me

growing. The primitive need to make sure of her, to make sure she's mine and mine alone.

She ignores me. 'My brother is in love. He just told me.'

But I don't care about Ulysses Zakynthos. For the first time since my parents died, I don't care about him at all. The only thing that matters is the woman in front of me and the fact that she hasn't gone after all. She's here. She chose me in the end, not him.

'Do as I say,' I growl.

Again, she ignores me. 'He let her go because of me. So I told him he was an idiot and that he needed to go and find her.'

'I don't care about your damn brother,' I grit out, pulling her even closer, the press of her soft body making me even harder than I am already. 'What I care about is you getting naked.'

She doesn't resist, but she doesn't obey either. 'Don't you see, Rafael? He's in love and he's going to get the woman he loves. He's probably going to marry her if she'll have him, and I think he'll have children with her too.'

'I don't give a fuck about him,' I snarl, my fingers tightening on her hips, pulling the heat between her thighs hard against my aching groin.

'You should,' she says in the same tone of voice she's said everything. 'Because it'll mean I'm not his heir any more.'

In some dim recess of my brain, I know that should mean something to me, but I can't think why it's important right now, not when she's here, right against me and she's so warm, so delicious.

I want her. I want her so badly I can't think. She almost left me, almost walked away, and all I can think about is claiming her, right here, right now. So she'll never walk away again.

'Take off your dress,' I order viciously. 'Now.'

CHAPTER EIGHTEEN

Olympia

RAFAEL'S DARK EYES look black despite the sunshine coming through the windows and the lines of his face are taut. His fingers are digging into my hips and he looks as if he's been pushed beyond all endurance. He must be if the prospect of me not being Ulysses's heir doesn't matter to him.

In contrast to the tension pulled to singing point in him, I feel a curious sense of freedom in myself. It's as if I've been wearing shackles, and I didn't realise, and now they've fallen off, and I feel so light I could almost rise into the air and fly.

I've always hated how much of a tie I was to Ulysses, how he made me a monument to his guilt and how I resented being his responsibility. Yet I hadn't realised how heavy my own feelings of responsibility have been towards him.

Because I did feel responsible for him. For how his life had wound around mine, the both of us growing together so tightly that we didn't have lives of our own. But now he has someone else, someone he loves desperately, I saw the glow and pain of it in his eyes, and all I feel is happiness for him that he's found someone. Someone who can give him all the love and joy he deserves, and who isn't bound up in his own failure the way I am. And now I feel free in a way I've never felt before. Ulysses has gone to reclaim a life for himself, and I need to do the same for me.

Except while I feel free from the bonds my brother inadvertently laid on me, my life is now bound inextricably with that of the man standing in front of me. Who is gripping me so hard it's as if he's afraid I'll disappear if he lets go.

He's fierce and intense, and desperate. For years he's been following this one goal, this dream of revenge, and now that I've taken it away from him he doesn't know what to do.

I was furious with him for not telling me that Ulysses was coming and for making it so clear that he'd never had any intention of dropping his plans. That he didn't listen to me, that he didn't care what I wanted, and the ghost of that anger is still there. Except now I'm looking up into Rafael's eyes and I see his desperation and his fury, and I realise suddenly where it comes from.

He said he thought I'd go with Ulysses and I can see that he truly believes that. He really did think I'd go with my brother and that made him afraid. Why else would he be this furious and demanding? He's a man who cares and cares deeply, and now I wonder if he feels that for me.

He certainly stayed where he was as I told him to,

despite his fear that I would leave. He didn't come out, didn't try to stop me, even when I hugged my brother. It cost him, though, I can see that so clearly. It cost him to stay here, to let me make a choice, and I realise that now: it *was* a choice I could have made. I could have gone with Ulysses, but I didn't. I stayed here. Because of Rafael.

He obviously hasn't registered that I'm likely to be Ulysses's heir no longer, or, if he has, it truly doesn't matter to him. Why was he so afraid I'd leave? Why did it matter that I choose him over my brother? Is it just because of the baby? Or is it about something more?

Ignoring his command, I stare up into his dark eyes. 'I was never going to go with him, Rafael. I was always going to stay here with you.'

A muscle leaps in his strong jaw. 'Why? Because of the child?'

'Not only that. I promised you I'd stay, remember? That I'd live with you, be your wife.'

'And if you weren't pregnant?' he demands. 'Would you stay then?'

There's a desperate note in his deep voice and I realise suddenly. Of course, he's wondering the same things I am. 'You mean, would I stay for you?' I ask.

His gaze is edged as an obsidian blade. 'Yes.'

It costs him to admit this too, I can see. And he's afraid of the answer.

You're afraid, too.

I am, but if I'm tired of hiding, I'm also tired of being afraid. Tired of locking away all my emotions, of putting up a facade. Of worrying about someone else's feelings, when all I want is to embrace my own. So I give him the answer I'm afraid of, the one that has been locked deep inside me ever since we met. 'I would stay for you,' I say. 'Even if we didn't have a child.'

The flames in his eyes leap and a savage smile twists his mouth. His fingers on my hips firm and I can feel the press of him through the fabric of my dress, hard and hot and ready. 'Then do as I say, dragonfly. Take off your dress and prove it to me.'

There's raw need in his voice and it tugs at my heart and makes me ache. When has anyone ever needed me the way Rafael needs me? For my brother I was something to be protected and kept wrapped in cotton wool. I didn't give him anything, I only took from him. I was a source of fear and guilt, and nothing I did made any difference. But I can make a difference to Rafael. I can be more than a source of fear and guilt. I can be a source of comfort and pleasure, and I want to be. For him, I want to be. He's lost everyone he ever loved, everyone who mattered to him, and he's still grieving. But he hasn't lost me. I'm here. I'm here for him.

But that's not all you want.

No, it's not. I knew it the moment I saw my brother's face. There was a light inside him when he told me that he'd met someone, and I knew immediately that he was in love. I told him that he was free of me now, that he had to go get the woman he loved. I told him that I was happy and that he needed to find his own happiness, but… I lied to him.

I'm not happy. Because Rafael has told me that love will not be a part of our marriage, and I thought I was okay with it. I thought it didn't matter, but watching Ulysses leave to find the woman who captured his heart has made me realise that I want that too. I don't want a marriage without love. I don't.

That's not the worst part, though. The worst part is that I'm starting to realise that the person I want to find love with is my husband. A man still in agony from the love he lost and who doesn't want another.

'Let me go,' I say softly.

He doesn't want to, I can see that, yet his hands fall away all the same. That muscle flicks in his jaw, the lines of his tall, powerful figure taut.

A heavy, dense silence falls between us and I can feel the distance in it. A distance that's growing wider and wider no matter how much I don't want it to be there.

'I don't think I can do this, Rafael.' I have to force myself to say the words.

The look in his eyes flares, a fleeting agony then gone. His expression hardens like stone. 'What the hell are you talking about?'

'I'm talking about us,' I say. 'You and me.'

One of his hands has curled into a fist and his mouth is hard. 'What about you and me? You're my wife now, Olympia. You can't say you can't do this, not half an hour after we got married.'

A thread of shame creeps through me, because he's right. My wedding vows were a promise and I'm breaking them already, and it's not fair. Not when he already told me that love couldn't and wouldn't be a part of our marriage. It's not as if I wasn't warned. And yet…

Ulysses has gone off to claim a life of his own and I want to claim mine. I want love too, yet I'm afraid. Horribly afraid of asking for it, of demanding it.

Ulysses has to love me—I'm his sister—but Rafael doesn't. I'm his in every possible way, but I want him to be mine, too. I have chosen him, but has he chosen me? That night in Singapore he seduced me for revenge, then he kidnapped me for our child. Now he's demanding I stay because I'm his wife, but is any of that about *me*? Or am I merely a symbol for him the way I was for Ulysses?

I don't want to be a symbol or a monument, or a doll kept in a high cupboard. I want to be a woman. I want to be loved for myself, not for what I represent, and I want to be loved in return.

I lift my chin. 'I know. And it's unfair of me when you told me very clearly what our marriage will be. But…my brother is in love, Rafael. And I…want that for me. I want that for us.'

His expression hardens even more, his features carved from granite. 'I told you, I don't want any part of that.'

I swallow, my mouth dry, my heart aching. I should stop talking and accept what we have now, not ask for more, and after all, who's to say we might not have it one day? Given time?

But deep down inside me, I know that to accept it would be a lie, and I can't lie to Rafael.

What are you going to do, then? Leave him? Take his child away from him? How selfish would that make you?

Is it selfish? To want love? To require it from someone? To possibly throw away what I have now just because he won't love me? Then again, what kind of marriage would we have without that? And what kind of environment would that be like for our child? And do I really want to risk it?

'Why not?' I ask him straight out. 'Would it be so very bad?'

He looks away from me a moment, that muscle in the side of his jaw flicking and leaping. 'I loved my father,' he says into the weighty quiet. 'I told you that, and I thought he loved me. I thought he loved my mother too.' Rafael glances back at me, his gaze like black ice. 'But in the end he chose his own humiliation, his own pain, and he left us to pick up the pieces.'

My throat closes at the anger and bitterness in Rafael's voice, and at the pain that lurks beneath them. He didn't listen last night, did he? Not to a word I said. 'Rafael,' I begin.

'I found him,' he goes on, ignoring me. 'He was in the study. He didn't even have the forethought to shoot himself somewhere else where I wouldn't have to see it. No, he did it in his study and I found him by his desk.'

There is so much fury in his voice. It makes my throat ache.

'My mother was devastated. She loved him so much, but in the end, her love wasn't enough to make him stay either. She had to sell herself after that, just so we could get by.' His gaze sharpens like razor blades. 'And not long after that, they found a tumour in her lungs. She died very quickly, which was the only mercy she found. But love didn't save her. Love didn't pay our debts or put food on our table. Love was only a terrible pressure, that ground us both into dust, and after she died, I decided that love would never be part of my life ever again.'

I don't know what to say to that. All I have is my own truth. 'Love saved me,' I say simply. 'Ulysses saved me.'

'And he trapped you, too,' Rafael says. 'Because he loved you. Why would you willingly give yourself up to that again?'

Again, I have no answer. But even if I did, he wouldn't listen anyway so what's the point?

Another silence falls once more. It's suffocating.

Then Rafael moves, stepping up to me, looking down into my face. 'We don't need it, dragonfly,' he says roughly. 'Not when we have this.' His hands land on my hips, his fingers curling into the fabric of my dress, pulling it up.

My heartbeat is already racing, my skin sensitised, and I can feel the pressure build between my thighs. I don't protest as he pulls my dress up, raising my arms so he can pull it off and over my head.

I should stop him, stand my ground and demand what I want, but I'm tired of demanding that too. I'm tired of fighting, of not being listened to. Maybe he's right. Maybe we don't need love. Maybe the way he makes me feel physically is all that I need.

'I won't trap you,' Rafael murmurs in my ear as he reaches around to unsnap the clasp of my bra. 'I won't be like him.' He pulls the straps down my arms and off, then he pushes down my knickers. 'I'll set you free.'

His hands slide over my bare skin, taking away all the constricting fabric binding my body, and as it slides away, I realise he's right. He *does* set me free. Because that's how I feel now, naked but for my wedding ring. So, do I really need more than this?

He sweeps me up in his arms, carries me over to the sofa and puts me down on it, then, with calm and methodical movements, he strips off his own clothes until he's finally as naked as I am. Then he stretches himself over me and I'm spreading my legs, welcoming him as he settles between them. I slide my hands up his muscular arms, caressing his smooth, velvety olive skin, moving up to his wide, strong shoulders and stroking them too. He looks into my eyes, easing one hand between my thighs, touching me, stroking me, testing me. There are black flames in his gaze and they're all-consuming, and a small part of me, the one that still doubts, feels a spark of fear. Wondering if it's too late for me. Too late not to want more. Too late for my heart to remain mine.

I'm afraid for the heart that beats so hard every time he looks at me. For the way I feel when he touches me, free and powerful and strong.

His intensity and his passion are a magnet I can't escape, a light I'm irresistibly drawn to like a moth to a flame, and I don't have the strength to fight it, not any more.

His dark gaze searches my face as if he's imprinting it on his memory, noting every change of expression as his fingers stroke me, exploring the wet folds of my sex, making me shiver and gasp. 'You chose me,' Rafael murmurs. 'Didn't you, dragonfly? You chose me.'

'Yes,' I gasp as he slides a finger inside me. 'Oh… yes…'

'And you'll never leave me, will you?' He adds another finger, stretching me, driving me insane. 'Not ever.'

'No…' I lift my hips, my thinking beginning to unravel. Everything beginning to unravel. Why would I leave him when he can make me feel this good?

'You don't need anything more than this,' he whispers, his hand moving slowly, in and out, making me writhe. 'Only me, touching you.'

I shudder, the smoky, musky scent of him filling my head, his touch everything, and I know he's right. All I need is this, his hands on me, his body close to mine, and pleasure… Pleasure everywhere.

He takes his hand from between my thighs and raises it, easing his fingers into my mouth. 'This is how you taste when I touch you,' he says, his voice rough velvet. 'No one else can give you this. Only me, your husband.' He removes his fingers and licks them, his gaze a hot knife right through me. 'You're part of me now, dragonfly.' The words are a soft growl. 'You're inside me and you can't ever escape.'

But I don't want to escape. I don't ever want to. I want to stay right here with him.

He shifts, pushing inside me, going slowly, methodical and careful now. He slides deep, making me gasp, then he pauses, looking down into my eyes.

He's deep inside me, surrounding me, his shadowed

gaze the whole world, then he slides his hands behind my knees, lifting them over his hips. I wrap them around his waist, holding him even as he holds me, allowing him to slide even deeper.

'I will give you everything,' he murmurs, and I can hear the vow in his voice, see it in the glittering of his onyx eyes. 'I will never hurt you, I promise. You'll always be safe with me.'

He means it, I can hear his fierce will burning in every word, yet that voice in the back of my head is whispering again. Whispering that I'm not safe, that he will hurt me at some point, because it's too late. It's too late to walk away from him, too late to escape him.

He was right when he said he wouldn't trap me, that he'd set me free. He did, only I didn't leave when I should have. I stayed and now it's too late, because I have a horrible feeling that I've trapped myself.

Because I'm falling in love with him.

But I can't think about that now, not now he's moving inside me and making me gasp. Making me clutch him, dig my fingers into his strong shoulders. Making me scream his name as we go down together in flames.

CHAPTER NINETEEN

Rafael

THE HANDPICKED TEAM of builders I got in to help me with Olympia's studio have left for the day, and now I'm standing in front of the structure, going over it with an expert eye. It's been years since I've taken an active part in building anything—I leave that to my construction teams usually—but Olympia's studio is different.

This is a special place for her and her alone, and so I wanted to help build it myself. I would have done the whole thing myself—it's not as if I've forgotten how to construct a building—but I wanted to finish it fast so she can use it before the baby arrives, which meant getting in a team to help.

They've just put the roof on and we celebrated with beers all round, then I sent them home. My hands are dirty and rough from fitting wooden beams and nailing struts, but there's a deep satisfaction inside me, the kind that comes from creating something, from building something concrete.

Something for her.

Months have passed since she chose me over her

brother and I don't recall ever being happier. I don't think about Ulysses Zakynthos. I don't think about my revenge or my lost family, or my father's blood on the floor of his study, not when she is all I think about. And certainly not when the arrival of our child is imminent.

Yet no matter how happy I am, I can't escape the feeling that all of this is somehow…fragile. There are times when I catch Olympia's gaze on me, something in it I can't name, a kind of despair that makes my breath catch. It's fleeting though, there one minute, gone so fast the next that I can almost tell myself I didn't see it. I certainly don't want to ask her about it. I don't want anything to burst this little soap bubble we're living in.

After our marriage, I took her on a honeymoon back to Singapore and we managed to get some sightseeing in—when we brought ourselves to leave our hotel suite, of course. We've gone on a few other trips since then, because she wanted to do some travelling before the baby is born. We went to China, Japan, and then to the States, because I have an office in New York and thought she might like to see the Big Apple.

It was only after returning to Sicily that I thought I'd better start on the studio so she will have a place of her own to retreat to. Also, while I have a big workshop space, the jewellery-making equipment I bought for her is taking over and we really need it to have its own space.

The studio is coming along nicely and now we have the roof on, I can concentrate on the interior. I'm going to make her cabinets and shelves so she has all the storage space she needs, lots of little places to put things.

Just then, I hear a step on the brick path that winds from the house to where the shell of the studio stands, and I turn.

Olympia is coming towards me. Her hair is loose today, lying over her shoulders in a thick, glossy black waterfall, and she's wearing a dress of blue silk that alternately billows then clings as she walks, outlining the dramatic curve of her stomach. She's nearly nine months now and our child will be here at any minute. Every time I look at her, I feel a complex mix of intense excitement and fear. I want to wrap her up, keep her safe and protected, yet I also want her with a savage need that borders on obsession.

'The roof is on,' I tell her, gesturing to the studio. 'I'm going to start on the interior tomorrow.'

She glances at the studio briefly and then looks back at me. Her eyes are glittering and there's something tense in her expression. Concerned, I come over to her. 'What is it, dragonfly?'

She gives me a very odd, tight smile. 'Ulysses has asked Katla to marry him. They'll be getting married in Reykjavik at Christmas time.'

I search her face. Surely this is wonderful news? I haven't taken any notice of Ulysses in the past six months, though sometimes Olympia tells me what he's doing. He's invited her back to Athens several times, but Olympia has always refused. I'm not sure why. I've long since lost the fear that she'll go back to him, and I wouldn't stop her if she wanted to go. Not that she'd let me.

I frown at her expression, reaching out to pull her close. 'That's good news, isn't it?'

'Yes, I suppose so.' Her voice has a slight edge to it. 'Except the timing isn't great.'

'Why not?' I ask. 'You'll have had the baby by then, and there's nothing to say we can't travel.'

Her eyes are still glittering and her cheeks are pink. '"We"?'

'Yes, of course "we".' My frown deepens. Are those tears? 'Something's upset you. What is it?'

She blinks and, yes, there are tears caught like diamonds on the ends of her lashes. She's staring at me as if she's never seen me before. 'You really want to attend his wedding?'

'Not for him,' I clarify. 'But I will for you.'

She continues to stare at me, then abruptly, she looks away. 'You're making this so difficult.' Her voice is so soft I almost don't hear.

'What?' I ask, a cold sensation settling in my gut.

'Nothing.' She pulls away from me and swipes a quick hand across her face. 'It's just…they didn't get to come to our wedding.'

This time I'm the one staring at her. Something's upsetting her and it's not Ulysses's wedding, I'm certain. It's something else.

'Olympia.' I reach for her again, because I know she finds my touch reassuring. 'Tell me what's wrong.'

She doesn't look at me and something shifts deep inside me, that sense of fragility, of precariousness. For the past few months things have been good. No, they've been perfect and I've been telling myself that's what our life will be like from now on. Yet, there's a part of me that knows something is missing and that I'm lying to myself about it.

Olympia is happy, I'm sure she is. If I don't want to acknowledge those moments when I see despair in her eyes. Or the times when I feel she's pulling away from me, a distance between us I can't bridge.

I reach out and grab her chin, bringing her gaze back to mine. 'What is it, dragonfly? You can tell me anything, you know that, don't you?'

She swallows and the tears in her eyes overflow. 'Stupid pregnancy hormones,' she mutters, trying to pull away.

But I won't let her, the doubt inside me growing, a cold, sharp fear. 'Is it the baby?'

She shakes her head, her lashes lowering. The tears slide slowly down her cheeks and my chest tightens, an unbearable pressure squeezing me. 'It's not the baby,' she says. 'The baby is fine.'

'Then what is it?' I can't stop the rough edge of demand entering my voice. I hate to see her cry. I hate to see her in any kind of pain at all.

Her lashes lift, her golden eyes liquid. 'It's you.'

Shock slides through me. 'What?' I ask blankly, not understanding.

'It's you, Rafael. I told myself it would be okay, that time would help. That time might even be the cure or the antidote or…or something. But…it just hasn't helped.'

I still don't understand. 'What are you talking about?'

She is silent a moment, then says, 'I'm in love with you.'

And I blink, another wave of shock sliding like ice down my back.

'I tried to tell myself that being here with you was enough,' she goes on, her voice cracking. 'I tried to tell myself that perhaps with time I'd either stop loving you or that…that maybe you'd change your mind about me. But that hasn't happened and now…' She takes a breath. 'Now, my brother is marrying the woman he loves and. I… I lied to him. I told him I was happy and I'm not.'

The shock is slowly dissipating and yet it still feels as if I've been struck by something heavy and my head is ringing.

Of course you can't make her happy. You're denying her what you know she needs. What you know she deserves.

Love. The one thing I didn't want. The one thing I told her wouldn't be a part of our marriage. I knew what I was denying her, I knew it. But I told myself that if I gave her whatever she wanted, a life of her own and all the pleasure she needed to fill it, she'd never need anything more. That I could make her happy with that alone.

But I can see the tears streaming down her cheeks and I can feel the distance between us widening even further. And I can't follow her. I can't.

Didn't you think this might be a problem? Didn't it ever enter your head?

No. I didn't want to think about it so I didn't.

'What can I do?' I hear myself say. 'What can I do to make you happy?'

'I don't know.' She swipes at her tears again and I try to do it for her, but she pulls away, putting some physical distance between us. 'There's nothing you can do.' She takes a breath, then another, and looks at me again. 'It's fine. Forget I ever said anything.'

CHAPTER TWENTY

Olympia

RAFAEL IS LOOKING at me, a stunned expression on his face. And of course he's stunned. I've never told him that I'm in love with him. I've kept that secret to myself for months now, hoarding it as a dragon hoards gold. And they've been wonderful months, too, the best of my life. I probably could have gone on without telling him, gone on with yet more wonderful months, but when Ulysses called me to tell me that he was marrying Katla, all I could think about was the lie I told him. The lie that I've been telling him for months now.

He asks me every so often, on our frequent calls, if I'm happy and is Rafael treating me well, and I tell him that I am and that Rafael couldn't be more attentive. That, at least, wasn't a lie. Rafael has been amazing. Taking me travelling and showing me some of his favourite places. They're all buildings, of course. The Great Wall in China. The Empire State in New York. The temples in Japan. He's passionate about them and while we've been away, he's been drawing more. Not only buildings either, but people, too. Me in particular.

Lying there watching him draw me is one of my life's pleasures, and one I don't want to give up. I don't want to give up any of it. I don't want to give up him, not for even a minute. Ulysses has asked me to visit him a number of times, but I've always refused. Some part of it is not wanting to be away from Rafael, but mostly it's because my brother will know that I've been lying to him. And he'll want to know why, and if I tell him, he'll probably fly straight to Sicily and wring Rafael's neck.

Perhaps I would have gone on that way if Ulysses hadn't mentioned the wedding. Making me think about my own marriage and the man I married. The man I'm desperately in love with, but I didn't want to tell him. Because I know he doesn't want it and I was terrified of what he'd do if I let him know.

But fear is what I'm trying to leave behind me, along with the pretence that everything's okay when it's not.

He is standing in front of the studio he built me, the building looking amazing and yet somehow also eclipsed by the man in front of it. A man in jeans and a black T-shirt, both stained with sweat and dust. His hands are dirty and there's blood on his fingers from a cut, and his hair has been shoved back from his head, and he's the most beautiful human I've ever seen. And I couldn't stop the words, they just came tumbling out.

Our child will be born very soon and I had to tell him before that happened. I had to be honest and I had to be strong. But while it was cathartic to say it, I regret it now, and I know that no matter how many times I tell him to forget it, he's not going to.

His eyes are very dark, his expression slowly hardening. 'It's not fine,' he says harshly. 'And no, I can't forget it.'

I swallow, because now it's here, what I dreaded would happen if I told him, and I can't run away from the consequences. I've been running from them for six months and I can't do it any longer.

'Okay,' I say. 'Well, now you know.'

He's staring at me as if I'm a stranger. 'Why would you tell me that?'

I straighten and lift my chin, drawing the shreds of my dignity around me and ignoring the pain threatening to crack me apart. 'Because I'm tired of hiding it,' I say baldly. 'And I'm not ashamed of it.'

'Olympia—'

'I'm not asking anything of you,' I interrupt, because now my secret's out, I won't let him stop me from speaking. 'I don't want anything. I'm not going to leave you just because you don't love me back or anything, and I don't want you to feel as if I'm pressuring you to give me something. I… I just needed to say it. And I needed you to hear it.'

He blinks as if I've shocked him again. 'What do you mean you don't want anything?'

'What? Did you expect me to turn my back and leave in a huff? How can I do that when I'm nine months pregnant, for God's sake? No, I'm not leaving. We're having a baby very soon and I'm not letting love get in the way of that. We can go on the way we've been going. It doesn't change anything.'

He only stares at me as if I'm speaking in a completely different language. 'Of course it changes things,' he says, suddenly forceful. 'It changes *everything*.'

'How?' I throw the question back at him. 'Why does knowing that I love you matter?'

He takes a couple of steps towards me then stops and stands there, rigid. His expression blazes with shock and fury, his eyes glittering. 'I want you to be happy,' he says through gritted teeth. 'I have been doing *everything* to make you happy.'

'Oh? So this is my fault?' I take a couple of steps towards him, because if he's going to get angry with me for that, I'll get furious right back. 'Don't you dare throw this back on me. You can't expect me to live with you, sleep at your side, accept all the gifts you shower me with and all the things you do for me, and have me *not* fall in love with you.' I take another step. 'What did you think would happen, you stupid bastard? I didn't want to fall in love with you. It just happened!'

His furious gaze matches mine and I'm surprised sparks aren't flying at the contact. 'Why?' His voice is hoarse. 'Why can't you be satisfied with what I have to give?'

'I am!' I shout. 'But didn't you listen to me? Didn't you hear when I told you that I don't want anything from you? You never listen, Rafael. Just like you didn't listen when I told you that it's okay to keep loving your father!'

'I heard.' His hands come out and he's gripping my upper arms so hard it's almost painful. 'This isn't about my father,' he snarls. 'This is about us. About what you want from me and you *should* want more from me. You should want *everything* from me.'

'Tell me what the point of that would be, Rafael. When you won't give it to me.'

He takes a shuddering breath, and there's something agonised in his eyes. 'You should leave me,' he says. 'You should turn around and walk away. You should find someone else.'

'Why should I? When I've already made my choice? A choice you made damn sure of nine months ago.'

He releases me suddenly and steps back. His face has gone white. 'Olympia…'

It's wrong of me to blame him for it, to bring up his stupid revenge plan, but I can't help it. I'm hurt. I'm in pain, and I'm angry. I should never have told him, but I did, and now I've ruined everything. We can't come back from this, I know we can't.

I turn to leave and that's when my waters break.

CHAPTER TWENTY-ONE

Rafael

I'M STILL IN shock and anger is coursing through my veins, and I shouldn't have said the things I said. I shouldn't have blamed her for loving me, not when it's myself I'm furious with. Furious that I didn't think her own heart would be at risk. Furious that I thought that denying her the one thing she deserved would be enough. Furious that gifts and studios and pleasure aren't enough, that she wants more.

She doesn't want more. She told you that. She's not demanding anything of you. And she's right. You don't listen.

That thought is still echoing in my head when she stops dead in her tracks and I see fluid running down her legs and onto the ground. And everything inside me seizes.

She's shivering as she turns to look at me, her golden eyes wide with fear. And all my fury vanishes as if it's never been. She's looking at me as if she needs me, and, no matter what I feel now, nothing is more important than her and our baby in this moment.

I move towards her and pick her up in my arms. 'It's all right,' I murmur as I stride towards the house. 'I'm here and I'm calling the doctor.'

She doesn't fight me, turning her head and burying it in my chest as we enter the house. Then everything moves very quickly. I call the private obstetrician who is managing her pregnancy. We both decided that we wanted our child to be born here, and from the looks of Olympia, we probably wouldn't have the time to go elsewhere anyway. The doctor is on her way, so I get my dragonfly into a hot shower to warm her up, then bundle her up on our bed. I hold her tightly as she trembles and for some reason start telling her stupid stories about my own childhood here and how I got into trouble all the time and how long-suffering my parents were.

She doesn't laugh at my pathetic attempts to cheer her, but when I fall silent, she says, 'Keep talking.'

So I do and the memories come. And like that Christmas night under the tree, they're not painful. They're good memories, happy memories, and far more of them than I thought, and something inside me loosens.

I keep talking when the doctor finally arrives and I keep talking as she examines Olympia and then gives me some instructions about what to do next. Apparently our baby is on its way, and I'm terrified. But this is one situation where I'm happy to let the doctor order me around until I'm finally holding my dragonfly as our baby is born.

'It's a girl,' the doctor says, beaming as she quickly

wraps my daughter up and sets her on Olympia's stomach. And I look down at the tiny creature wrapped up in white muslin. Her little face is all screwed up and she looks so angry, and it fills me then, the most intense feeling I've ever had in my life. A force so strong and pure and right that I can't deny it.

Olympia has gathered her into her arms and I stare like a fool at the pair of them. And I realise that the feeling isn't just for my daughter. It's for the woman who gave birth to her, who created her. The woman who has stayed with me for six months, loving me, and who even when I told her to leave, didn't.

It's been there a long time, that feeling.

'Call Ulysses,' Olympia says to me. 'Tell him he's an uncle.'

'You don't want to?' I ask stupidly.

She shakes her head, her attention on our daughter.

I don't want to leave and yet I move out of the room, fumbling for my phone, my hands shaking. The doctor is talking to Olympia now and she doesn't need me any more. Our baby is born.

Out in the hallway, I hit the number for Ulysses and wait, still dazed.

'Zakynthos,' he answers.

All thought goes out of my head. For years I've wanted revenge on this man and that was all I could think about but now... Now I've even forgotten why I was so angry with him in the first place.

Your father. Your mother. Remember?

Ah yes, that's right. Revenge. But it feels so distant now, the anger that drove me. And after recounting all those happy childhood stories to Olympia, it doesn't even feel like me.

'You have a niece,' I say hoarsely.

There's a silence and then he says, 'Santangelo?'

'Yes.'

'Olympia, how is—'

'She's well. She's fine and so is the baby.'

Another silence.

'Have you been forbidding her from seeing me?' he asks.

It's a question I'm not expecting. 'No,' I say, my brain still feeling sluggish and slow. 'No, I didn't.'

'Then why doesn't she visit?'

But I know the answer to that and I find myself saying, to my enemy, 'Because she doesn't want you to know that she's unhappy.'

'If you have hurt her,' Zakynthos snarls down the phone, 'I will personally cut out your heart and feed it to you.'

I shut my eyes, a curious, deep pain radiating through me. 'I'm sorry,' I hear myself say. 'I should never have taken her. I should never have even touched her.'

'No,' he says tersely. 'You shouldn't have. But you did and so here we are. Now. Why is she unhappy?'

It's a valid question and I have to answer. 'Because she loves me.'

Another silence, even longer this time.

'And you don't love her?' he asks. 'Be very, very careful how you answer.'

I swallow, my mouth dry, my heart like a drum in

my chest. And I open my mouth to say no, but even as I go to shape the word, I know it's a lie. It was a lie six months ago and it's a lie still. I *do* love her. I've loved her since the moment I saw her in a red gown with a dragonfly clip in her hair in Singapore, and I have no idea what to do about it.

Love wasn't something I ever wanted to involve myself with again, because I know how it can rip your life apart. How once given, you can't take it back, no matter how badly you want to. And how in the end, even after you've given up everything for it, it's still not enough.

'I do love her,' I say, my voice still hoarse. 'But...'

'But what?' he says impatiently.

And I realise then that I have to think about this, that I can't just push it aside for once. That the question of love isn't about what I do and don't want, it's about fear. My fear.

'I'm afraid,' I say slowly, knowing even as I do that admitting a vulnerability to this man is a mistake. 'I'm afraid it's not enough. That I won't be able to make her happy.'

And it's true. My very existence wasn't enough to stay my father's hand when he picked up that gun, and as for my mother, she was too bound up in grief to think about me. And I was their son. So what am I to Olympia? The man who got her pregnant, kidnapped her, forced her into marriage, and who made her stay here in my villa, with my baby. Who made her love him.

I've trapped her as surely as her brother once did, and, worse, I want to deny her the only thing she's never asked me for. And all because I'm too afraid to give it.

'Well, that's bullshit,' Zakynthos says, brutally frank. 'You have a child now and a woman who loves you, and whether you're afraid or not, that's what you have. So stop being a coward. Your only job now is to spend the rest of your life at least trying to make her happy or I'll gut you like a fish.' He ends the call abruptly, leaving me standing there staring at the wall like a fool.

He's right, though. Whether I'm afraid or not, I know now that there was never any leaving my dragonfly. And if she won't walk away, where does that leave me? I could give into my fear and walk away from her and our child, tell myself I'm setting her free of me, or…

Or I could stop lying to myself. Stop telling myself that I'm not afraid. Stop thinking that she's better off without me and I'm better off without her, because she's not. She *loves* me. I could see the fear in her eyes as she told me so, and yet she said it anyway, so how can I throw that back in her face? How can I be such a coward when she's the bravest person I've ever met?

That would do to her what my father did to me and I can't do that. I have to make a different choice, a better choice. She told me once that it's okay to love someone who hurt you, that it doesn't mean you forgive them, it's just an acknowledgement of what's in your heart, and finally now, I understand.

I can love my father and still be furious with him. And I can love my dragonfly and still be afraid. Because she's more important to me than my fear. She's more important than me entirely, and I can't walk away from her. I have to get over myself and be as honest with her as she was with me. After all, I have a wife who loves me and a child of my own, and that's more than some men ever get. It's certainly more than I deserve.

I turn and walk back into the bedroom.

Olympia is sitting back against the headboard, our daughter in her arms. She looks exhausted and very pale, but her eyes are glowing so bright it makes my heart hurt.

I sit on the bed beside her and as the doctor leaves, I meet her steady gaze. 'Don't leave me, dragonfly,' I say roughly. 'Please stay. Stay for me.'

Her brow creases. 'I'm not going anywhere, you idiot. I told you I wouldn't.'

I reach out and push a lock of hair behind her ear. 'I am an idiot,' I agree. 'Your brother told me that if I don't spend the rest of my life making you happy, he'll gut me like a fish.'

Her expression softens. 'You know I'm not going to demand that you—'

I reach out and lay a finger across her lovely mouth, silencing her. 'No. You need to demand it. You're right to demand it. Because you deserve it, dragonfly. And I...' I stop and take my finger away. 'I've been lying to you and lying to myself all this time. I told you love would never be part of our marriage, but even when I said it, there was a part of me that knew it was already too late. It was too late the moment I saw you in Singapore. I've been in love with you since then.'

She blinks, her eyes filling with sudden tears, and our daughter makes a soft sound as if responding to her mother's distress. But it's not distress, I can see that now. It's joy. And I realise that her brother was right. I really will dedicate the rest of my life to making her happy, because I want that joy. I want that joy of hers for ever.

'You were right,' I tell her, because I want her to know that I did listen. 'I did love Dad and I still do, but I can be angry at him as well. And I can love you and still be afraid that it might not be enough.'

Her smile is the second sweetest thing I've seen today, the first being our daughter. 'Of course it's enough,' she says huskily. 'You're here, aren't you? That's enough for me. That's all I ever wanted.'

My heart is painful inside me and it takes me a minute to understand that joy can be painful too, a beautiful, bittersweet pain. And I want to kiss her passionately, kiss her senseless, but she's just had our child and needs more care from me than that. So I satisfy myself with the softest, most gentle kiss I can give her and am rewarded with her sigh of pleasure.

'Do you want to hold our daughter, love?' she asks me as I lift my head, her eyes the most brilliant gold.

'Yes. I thought you'd never ask.'

So Olympia hands me our child, the warm weight of her settling into my arms. Her eyes are dark, like mine, but I swear she has a mouth just like her mother's.

I settle back beside my beautiful wife and as I do, I realise something.

After my parents died, I didn't really have a life. I only had revenge. But right here, right now, I do. And it starts with my dragonfly.

EPILOGUE

Olympia

THE CHRISTMAS TREE in the corner of the Icelandic lodge that Katla and Ulysses own is huge and the lights on it are twinkling, throwing beautiful colours all over the walls. I've hung up the reindeer ornament that Ulysses bought me last Christmas, the Christmas Rafael kidnapped me, and also the angel he bought me this year.

It's a tradition I've passed on to my husband, and now I stand there, holding our daughter, Elena, watching as Rafael hangs the Christmas ornament I made especially for him this year. It's a dragonfly, of course, and he was absolutely thrilled with it.

My little jewellery business has blossomed and grown, and this Christmas I decided to do a line of very special, very exclusive ornaments. It's taken off hugely, much to my surprise, and I ended up making a lot more than I anticipated. The dragonfly, though, is special. It's for him and him alone.

He has made his peace with Ulysses. After Elena was born, Ulysses took Rafael out to his hunting lodge in the mountains of central Greece, and they spent a few days 'working things out', or so Rafael said. They came back firm friends, having bonded over their shared involvement with crime families, and also after a knock-down, drag-out physical fight that neither won, but both felt much better after. Honestly, men.

Anyway, I love my sister-in-law, Katla, and she's sitting on the couch with my brother, the both of them looking like cats who have swallowed the cream.

I know why. Ulysses has told me that Katla is pregnant and I'm thrilled for them.

Elena makes a noise, her little arms reaching for her father, and after Rafael finishes hanging the dragonfly, he comes over to where I'm standing and takes our daughter into his arms. She makes happy sounds, patting her father's face while he looks down at her, absolutely besotted.

It makes my heart ache to watch them. It makes my heart ache to be here, with all the people I care about most in the world. Where there's nothing but joy and laughter, and love.

Love is what all of us need most of all.

* * * * *

If you couldn't put His Heir of Revenge *down, then be sure to check out the previous instalment in the Captured & Claimed duet,* Christmas Eve Ultimatum! *And why not try these other stories by Jackie Ashenden?*

Italian Baby Shock
The Twins That Bind
Boss's Heir Demand
Newlywed Enemies
King, Enemy, Husband

Available now!

Get up to 4 Free Books!

We'll send you 2 free books from each series you try PLUS a free Mystery Gift.

FREE Value Over **$25**

Both the **Harlequin Presents** and **Harlequin Medical Romance** series feature exciting stories of passion and drama.

YES! Please send me 2 FREE novels from Harlequin Presents or Harlequin Medical Romance and my FREE gift (gift is worth about $10 retail). After receiving them, if I don't wish to receive any more books, I can return the shipping statement marked "cancel." If I don't cancel, I will receive 6 brand-new larger-print novels every month and be billed just $7.19 each in the U.S., or $7.99 each in Canada, or 4 brand-new Harlequin Medical Romance Larger-Print books every month and be billed just $7.19 each in the U.S. or $7.99 each in Canada, a savings of 20% off the cover price. It's quite a bargain! Shipping and handling is just 50¢ per book in the U.S. and $1.25 per book in Canada.* I understand that accepting the 2 free books and gift places me under no obligation to buy anything. I can always return a shipment and cancel at any time. The free books and gift are mine to keep no matter what I decide.

Choose one:
- ☐ **Harlequin Presents Larger-Print** (176/376 BPA G36Y)
- ☐ **Harlequin Medical Romance** (171/371 BPA G36Y)
- ☐ **Or Try Both!** (176/376 & 171/371 BPA G36Z)

Name (please print)

Address   Apt. #

City   State/Province   Zip/Postal Code

Email: Please check this box ☐ if you would like to receive newsletters and promotional emails from Harlequin Enterprises ULC and its affiliates. You can unsubscribe anytime.

Mail to the Harlequin Reader Service:
IN U.S.A.: P.O. Box 1341, Buffalo, NY 14240-8531
IN CANADA: P.O. Box 603, Fort Erie, Ontario L2A 5X3

Want to explore our other series or interested in ebooks? Visit www.ReaderService.com or call 1-800-873-8635.

---

*Terms and prices subject to change without notice. Prices do not include sales taxes, which will be charged (if applicable) based on your state or country of residence. Canadian residents will be charged applicable taxes. Offer not valid in Quebec. This offer is limited to one order per household. Books received may not be as shown. Not valid for current subscribers to the Harlequin Presents or Harlequin Medical Romance series. All orders subject to approval. Credit or debit balances in a customer's account(s) may be offset by any other outstanding balance owed by or to the customer. Please allow 4 to 6 weeks for delivery. Offer available while quantities last.

Your Privacy—Your information is being collected by Harlequin Enterprises ULC, operating as Harlequin Reader Service. For a complete summary of the information we collect, how we use this information and to whom it is disclosed, please visit our privacy notice located at https://corporate.harlequin.com/privacy-notice. Notice to California Residents – Under California law, you have specific rights to control and access your data. For more information on these rights and how to exercise them, visit https://corporate.harlequin.com/california-privacy. For additional information for residents of other U.S. states that provide their residents with certain rights with respect to personal data, visit https://corporate.harlequin.com/other-state-residents-privacy-rights/.

HPHM25